THE VIRGINS

Also by Pamela Erens

The Understory

THE VIRGINS

Pamela Erens

JOHN MURRAY

First published in the United States of America in 2013 by Tin House Books

First published in Great Britain in 2014 by John Murray (Publishers)

An Hachette UK Company

1

A CIP catalogue record for this title is available from the British Library

Hardback ISBN 978-1-84854-987-6
Trade Paperback ISBN 978-1-84854-990-6
Ebook ISBN 978-1-84854-986-9

Printed and bound in Great Britain by Clays Ltd, St Ives plc

John Murray policy is to use papers that are natural, renewable and recyclable products and made from wood grown in sustainable forests. The logging and manufacturing processes are expected to conform to the environmental regulations of the country of origin.

John Murray (Publishers)
338 Euston Road
London NW1 3BH

www.johnmurray.co.uk

Once again for JDR, AER, and HER

1979

1

We sit on the benches and watch the buses unload. Cort, Voss, and me.

We're high school seniors, at long last, and it's the privilege of seniors to take up these spots in front of the dormitories, checking out the new bodies and faces. Boys with big glasses and bangs in their eyes, girls with Farrah Fawcett hair. Last year's girls have already been accounted for: too ugly or too studious or too strange, or already hitched up, or too gorgeous even to think about.

It's long odds, we know: one girl here for every two boys. And the new kids don't tend to come on these buses shuttling from the airport or South Station. Their anxious parents cling to the last hours of control and drive them, carry their things inside the neat brick buildings, fuss, complain about the drab, spartan rooms. If there's a pretty girl among them, you can't get close to her for the mother, the father,

the scowling little brother who didn't want to drive hundreds of miles to get here. We don't care about the new
boys, of course. We'll get to know them later. Or not.

She turns her ankle as she comes down the bus steps—
just a little wobble—laughs, and rights herself again. Her
sandals are tapered and high. Only a tiny heel connects with
the rubber-coated steps. She wears a silky purple dress, slit
far up the side, and a white blazer. Her outfit is as strange in
this place—this place of crew-neck sweaters and Docksid-
ers—as a clown's nose and paddle feet. Her eyes are heavily
made up, blackened somehow, sleepy, deep. She waits on
the pavement while the driver yanks up the storage doors at
the side. She points and he pulls out two enormous match-
ing suitcases, fabric-sided, bright yellow. His muscles bulge
lifting them onto the pavement.

I jump up. Cort and Voss are still computing, trying to
figure this girl out, but I don't intend to wait. Voss makes a
popping sound with his lips, to mock me and to offer his
respectful surprise. After all, I supposedly already have a
girlfriend.

"Do you need some help?" I ask her.

She smiles slowly, theatrically. Her teeth are very straight,
very white. Orthodontia or maybe fluoride in the water. I
wonder where she's from. City, fancy suburb? It suddenly
hits me. She's one of *those*. I can see it in her dark eyes, the
bump in her nose, her thick, dark, kinky hair.

"I'm in Hiram," she says.

Let me re-create her journey.

She awakens in her big room at an hour when it is still dark, pushes open the curtains of her four-poster bed. Little princess. Across the hall, her brother is still sleeping. He's four years younger than she is: twelve. She makes herself breakfast: a bagel with cream cheese, O.J., and a bowl of Cheerios; she's always ravenous in the morning. She eats alone. Her mother, in her bathrobe, reads stacks of journals upstairs. Her father is shaving. He doesn't like to eat in the morning. He brings her to the airport but they say nothing during the long drive through the flat gray streets of Chicago. She hopes that he'll say he'll miss her, that he'll pretend this parting takes something out of him. She was the one who asked to go away, but in the car her belly acts up, she's queasy. She thinks she may need to rush to the bathroom as soon as they get to O'Hare. She wishes she hadn't eaten so much. If her father would act like he might miss her, is afraid for her, she could be a little less afraid for herself. She has practiced her walk, her talk, everything she needs to present herself. She is terrified of going somewhere new simply to end up invisible again.

One long heel sinks into the mud. The past days have brought late-summer rains to New Hampshire, and although the air is now dry, the grass between the parking areas and the dormitories is soft and mucky. This is a girl used to walking on city pavement, concrete. She laughs and pulls herself out. She is determined to make it seem as if everything that happens to her is something she meant to happen, or can gracefully control. She avoids the wetter grass but in a moment she sinks again. "Oh boy," she says. Her dress is long, almost to her ankles. I put down her suitcases and hold out my hand; she takes it and I pull. Her freed shoe makes a sucking sound. When I go over the sound in my mind later, it strikes me as obscene. Her suitcases are heavy, heavy as I've since learned only a woman's luggage can be. It's only a little farther to her dorm. She tells me that she's an upper—what other high schools call a junior—and we exchange names. *Aviva Rossner*. She repeats mine, Bruce Bennett-Jones, like she's thinking it over, trying to decide if it's a good one.

She walks ahead of me instead of following, perhaps intending me to watch her small ass shifting under the white jacket. The wind lifts the hem of her dress, pastes it against her long bare leg. The Academy flag whips around above us and clings to the flagpole in the same way. The smell of ripened apples floods the air. We're on the pavement, finally; she click-clacks to the heavy door and opens it for me. Strong arms on such a slender girl. Someone's playing piano in the common room, a ragtime tune. Aviva starts up the stairs, expecting me to bring the bags. It's strictly against the rules for a boy to go up to the residential floors. I go up.

Inside the dorm, the light is dim. The walls are cream-colored and dingy, the floors ocher. She counts out the door numbers until she finds hers: 21. I put the suitcases by the dresser, the same plain wooden dresser that sits in my room and in every student room on campus. Her suitcases contain—we'll all see in the days to come—V-necked angora sweaters, slim skirts, socks with little pom-poms at the heels, teeny cutoff shorts, cowboy boots, lots of gold jewelry, many pouches of makeup.

There's a mirror above the dresser. I catch a view of my-self: sweaty forehead, damp curls. Aviva's roommate is not here yet. The closet yawns open, wire hangers empty.

"Thank you *so much*," she says.

I give the front door a push. It hits dully against the frame, doesn't shut. Aviva has plenty of time to do something: slip into the hallway, order me to go away. She regards me with a patient smile. I am going to slow down the action now, re-lating this; I want to see it all again very clearly. Like a play being blocked—my stock-in-trade. And so: I push again and the door grinding shut is the loudest and most final sound I have ever heard. Aviva steps back to lean against it and let me approach. She's a small girl and moving close to her I feel, for once, that I have some size. The waxy collar of her jacket prickles the hair on my forearms. Her neck is damp and slippery, and her mouth, as I kiss it, tastes like cigarettes and chocolate. I picture her smoking rapidly, fur-tively, in the little bathroom on the plane. Her hair smells a little rancid. The perfume she put on this morning has moldered with sweat and travel and now gives off an odor of decayed pear.

"Don't open your mouth so wide," she says.

My feet are sweating in my sneakers. My crotch itches. My scalp itches. She drops her hand and I see that her fin-gernails are painted a pearly pink.

She tilts her head against the door and laughs. Her thick curls swarm. I could bite her exposed neck. I do not want to get caught, sent home. I see my father's hand raised up to hit me and know I'm about to step off a great ledge. In a panic I reach for the doorknob, startling Aviva. I open the door carefully, listen to the stairs and hallways. "It's all right," she says, although how can she know this? But she happens to be correct. There's the oddest emptiness and silence as if these moments and this place were set aside just for us amid the busyness of moving-in day at the Academy. Aviva gives the door a bump with her ass to shut it again, but I insert myself into the opening and slide past her, fleeing down the stairs and out into Hiram's yard.

Cort and Voss are no longer sitting on the bench in front of Weld. A lone bicycle is chained to its arm.

Later I see Voss in the common room reading a *New Gods* comic book. "How was the chick?" he asks. I shrug. Big nose, I say. Too much makeup. Not my type.

2

It's late September, early October. Let's say October, that first week, the peak of foliage season. I see Aviva Rossner and Seung Jung meeting during that time, amid the flaming yellows and deep reds. Seung was a kid I knew from my New Jersey hometown; we'd been in middle school together. I don't really know when the two of them met, or how. One day she was simply there, Aviva, on the couch in our common room, sitting on his legs. He lay back, his head on the arm of the couch. She sat astride him, one leg dangling off the couch, the other bent beneath her. Her legs were bare; she had come from the gym. She wore gray gym shorts and a hooded sweatshirt that said AUBURN ACADEMY. His eyes were closed, he was smiling.

They meet in music theory. Let's say that. Aviva is always trying to broaden herself, to try things for which she has no aptitude: music theory, volunteering in the nursing home, drugs. She was afraid during her childhood and tried nothing, and now she wants to discover she is not really a coward. She sits in the big music room with the sheet-music stands pushed to the sides, listening to old Barnet Fretts with his muttonchops, his Down East accent. *Sing B flat*, he says. She cannot imagine B flat. How can one conjure it up from all the other tones? She sees the words *B flat* as if a typewriter were striking out the letters one by one. She tells herself that if she simply concentrates on those letters, the note that comes out of her mouth will be correct; her mind will find a way to arrange this. She sings her note. Old Fretts frowns.

Seung has the seat next to hers. The chairs are welded to scalloped desktops. He puts his hand on her arm. He is olive-colored, muscular, wearing a white Lacoste shirt with the required blazer and tie. A senior. "You have a nice voice," he says. It's true. She can't sing the right note but her voice is sweet. Seung's composition book is filled with tiny black notes like teardrops, inked carefully in his miniature, exact handwriting. When he tells her his name, she says it's perfect for this room, this hour: *Seung*, pronounced like the past tense of *sing*.

After class they walk together toward his dorm. It is on the way to her own. He knows who she is; he's watched her walk near him, past him, toward the library, up the stairs of the Assembly Building. Everyone knows who she is: she's that girl with the long, kinky hair and pale skin, the dark eye makeup, the V-neck sweaters that tease you into thinking you will catch a glimpse of her breasts. She wears high-heeled boots and gold hoop earrings. Another day, she might be costumed in the clothes that everyone else wears, turtlenecks and Fair Isle sweaters, but no one is fooled; she still doesn't look like anyone else.

She tries not to glance into the plate-glass windows of the art gallery as they pass. She finds it almost impossible to resist checking herself to make sure that she is sufficiently vivid, not fading away. She half expects, each time she looks, to see nothing there.

"What other classes are you taking?" Seung asks.

She wonders if she heard or only imagined a stutter on the word *taking*. Seung has short, thick legs, slightly bowed, a long, broad torso, and broad shoulders. His straight black hair, parted in the middle, completely covers his ears, grows past his chin. His face is a square. He gives an impression of intense physical strength, and Aviva soon learns that he swims butterfly on the varsity team. She has to look up to speak to him, though he is not especially tall. Tall maybe for an Asian kid. She is always having to look up. She compensates by standing back from other people, a little farther away than is natural. If you saw a photograph of her you would think she looked fragile—bony arms, narrow shoulders—but in person, something tough and irreducible overshadows that impression.

Seung is a proctor in his dorm, a position defined in the *Auburn Rule Book*, he tells Aviva, as *a liaison between the student body and the faculty on matters of student welfare and discipline.* "I try," he says, winking. He plays keyboard for a school band and loves jazz and a good old down and dirty rock-and-roll tune. The Southern groups are the best: Little Feat, Lynyrd Skynyrd, the Allman Brothers. They make you want to get up off your butt and dance.

"Are you from the South?" she asks. He doesn't seem it.

"New Jersey. Joisey. You're from the Midwest. Or Buffalo."

"Someone told you!" It does not surprise her that people should be talking about her.

"No. But you sound like those people you talk to when you order something from a catalog. They're all in Wisconsin or Chicago."

"What do you know about ordering from catalogs?"

"I got my mother a Lands' End sweater for her birthday. Korean mothers love Lands' End."

She tells him, almost proudly, that she has no talents whatsoever. She plays a little piano, badly. She can hit a tennis ball. She can't draw or paint. She likes to read, novels and psychology especially. She points to the library, the one built by the famous architect, with its brick piers and warm wood and many windows flooded with light. "I love that building," she says.

"I've seen you there," he tells her.

"Probably," she agrees. She often sits on the second floor in one of the big square armchairs, looking over the great lawn with its changing colors. She stays late. She doesn't like to be in her room; she and her roommate don't get along.

Her roommate won't lend out shirts or sweaters and doesn't approve of smoking. Every night the roommate carefully folds and hangs the clothes she has worn that day. She goes to bed early and wakes up early.

Aviva shifts her books to one side to make sure Seung gets a glimpse of her breasts, her waist. Already she has gathered that there's something resigned and self-doubting in his nature, something that makes it hard for him to think: *me*. If they part now, she will lose him.

"Are you taking anyone to the dance this Saturday?" she asks.

He expels a short, tight laugh. He's not. He rarely goes to the dances. He walks out to the woods with Detweiler and Sterne, his closest friends, occasionally with others from Weld, too. They smoke reefer or drop acid and listen to some goodness: Jean-Luc Ponty, Traffic, the Köln concert, with Keith Jarrett kicking the piano's footboard and moaning.

"Why don't you ask me?" she says.

3

I'm convinced that she made the first move, not the other way around. She'd had a few entanglements already; word had it that she came on strong. Then, after a week or two, she'd get tired of the guy, or maybe he'd decide it wasn't wholly an advantage to be linked to the new talked-about girl on campus. Anyway, my version fits with what I knew of Seung. Even back in middle school, when we pushed him up against the lockers and called him Chinky and Chinaboy, there were girls who liked him, and they liked him more as his shoulders broadened and his muscles hardened and he became one of the school's better athletes. But he never reached out for what he could get. Likewise at Auburn. He had his group of buddies, smart stoners and good-time guys mostly, but you rarely saw him with a girl. As if he didn't believe any of this female attention ran deep. He was waiting for someone to insist—to master him.

4

I'm inventing Seung, too, of course. It's the least I can do for him.

5

Four thirty, the grass darkening, the sky pressing near. Seung, Detweiler, and Sterne walk past the gym and the playing fields, which are emptying now, out to the track. The three friends look nothing alike. Detweiler is tall and skinny, with lank blond hair past his shoulders and granny glasses. His thoughts are always somewhere separate, tender; he smiles to himself without knowing it. No one likes to interrupt his reveries, which somehow gentle every gathering. Sterne is a different kind of thin: muscular, sinewy. He is a tennis player, shorter than Detweiler. His hair is dark, his cheeks hollowed. His family has loads of money and a ski cabin in Vermont. Next to these two, Seung looks like a weight lifter, a wrestler, a squat tree. They forget he is Asian, that his face stands out from theirs. He never forgets.

The track circles the soccer field. The boys crouch near one of the goalposts. Detweiler pulls out the narrow white joint, puts his lips to the end to seal it. If they had more time they might walk out to the Bog, where it's more secluded, better for a peaceful toke, but they have classes before dinner. Seung touches the joint with his lighter, and they pass it quietly. Seung watches the lanes, the way they nest inside each other, eight of them. He wishes he were out on the track the way he used to be, his chest bursting, smelling the sweat and sour breath of his nearest competitor, sensing that kid fall back while his own legs pumped on, stabbed with pain, unstoppable. He ran the 440 at Jordan Middle School: the hardest race, the one in which you can neither sprint nor spare yourself. His feet slammed against the packed dirt, he felt the vibrations up into his neck, his ears. In the eighth grade he injured his back and turned to swimming. A track is a repetition, circles, the same ground again and again. There is something comforting in that. Swimming offers Seung the same comfort: two walls, one channel between.

Sterne squints at the joint appreciatively. "California skunk—that's what this shit is called?"

"Why skunk?" asks Detweiler. He's got a hard-on. He always gets a hard-on when he tokes. It's just Detweiler. No one thinks to comment or not comment. His hand strays every so often to pat it thoughtlessly.

"Skunk because the indica cultivar smells like an effing skunk," says Seung. He's the guy with the technical information. "They cut it with a California strain, orange-flavored, so you don't barf. THC content seven to ten percent. I'm guessing this is a ten."

"Thank you, Mr. Chemistry," says Sterne.

They drink Coke from cans they bought in town, still cold to the touch. Sterne offers a package of almonds; they razz him for not bringing the roasted, salted kind.

"Hold still," says Seung to Sterne. "I'm going to draw you."

"Let me get comfortable," says Sterne. He takes off his jacket, plumps it under his head, and stretches out on his back.

"Don't close your eyes." Seung draws with a fine-nibbed pen, short tiny strokes like cross-hatching. His portraits never look much like the people they are meant to represent, but they capture something true nonetheless. His friends put these pictures away somewhere safe: beneath their socks, inside a cherished old book. Each thinks Seung has grasped something of his fussy complexity, the way he is made of a million little impulses and gestures.

The sun drops lower. Sterne's face is deeply in shadow. Seung begins to see Aviva lying there, head cushioned by the jacket, her dark hair snaking into the grass. He wants to take her out to the woods and seat her in a bed of pine needles, crouch by her and stroke her hair, touch her breasts, cup her hips. He has spoken to her only that once, in front of Weld. He is taking her to the dance on Saturday. Or is she taking him? His hands begin to shake. There's the sweet, cindery taste of the pot at the back of his throat. Last night he dreamt that he and Aviva were in the Academy pool with its marked-out lanes; he yanked the ropes away to give them room. The water beneath them was solid as a floor as he sank inside of her. When it was finished he was no longer a virgin.

He puts aside the drawing and takes something out of his pocket. Two days ago he noticed the loose baluster between the second and third floors of Weld. When no one was looking, he rattled it until it came free. He couldn't have said why he wanted it. He hid it in his room and, later, broke off the end, whittled off the jagged edges. The rest of the baluster he threw into the river, behind the boathouse. Now he begins to whittle again at the broken-off piece. He suddenly knows what he wants to make: a perfect sphere for Aviva. There will be no edges at all, no beginning or end, the same diameter in every direction. Not an oval, nothing lopsided. The wood—he thinks it is oak—is hard and has a fine grain. It will come up beautifully when polished.

"Five twenty," says Detweiler. He doesn't wear a watch but always knows what time it is.

They rise, groaning. Sterne has German at twenty of six; Detweiler, physics. Sterne can hardly keep his eyes open. Seung, in his role of proctor, is supposed to meet with a lower who has been cutting classes. I see the three walking back as I'm on my way to the Dramat, still shaking from my encounter with Aviva.

6

That's how I imagine things were, the afternoon I spoke to Aviva in the post office, during that lull after sports. The teams have come in from the fields. She wears a lavender sweater, cream-colored corduroys, clogs, and gold around her neck: two thin chokers plus another chain, longer, with a gold heart dangling from it. I am going to say that she has just come from the girls' bathroom, where she looked into the mirror and saw the blurred face that always frightened her. She thinks her features are ill defined, that she is too pale; the eyes of others will sweep over her and not linger. She pulls her makeup case out of her knapsack, darkens the lines ringing her eyes. She applies more mascara, more blush. She stands at different angles to the mirror, turning her head, stepping back, then coming very close. She cannot leave until her own image leaps out and startles her.

She pulls two slim letters from her mailbox. I have a letter from my father, Malcolm Bennett-Jones, Auburn class of '44, which will contain the usual admonitions. I ask who has written her. She answers me as if we've never met before. After my flight from her room I told myself I felt no attraction to her, that I found her *too*: too Jewish-looking, too artificial, too naked in her wish to be appreciated. But now that she's right in front of me, I feel the pull. Everything about her looks rich and strokeable.

"They're from my brother," she says.

"Both letters?"

"Yes."

She holds up one envelope so I can see the uneven, childish writing on the outside, the writing of a ten- or twelve-year-old.

"He must like you." I'm aware of my high voice, my damnable stature.

"I like him even better." She slides the letters into her copy of *Crime and Punishment*. We push past the others to get out and stand on the quadrangle.

"I could eat some ice cream," she says.

In Currie's Pizza on Main Street she eats ice cream from a cup with a pull-off lid, scraping at the surface with a tiny spoon. Boys in their blazers, ties loosened, watch her. The wooden tables are gouged with obscenities.

"What does your brother write about?"

"Oh, he tells me what books he's read, what they're teaching at school that he already knows. How the Cubs are doing. He's like an angel. He's always cheerful. My parents hate each other. Marshall is aware of everything, he understands it all, but it doesn't make him scared or mean. He told me not to feel guilty about leaving, that he would be fine. He knew I wanted to go."

"He's how old?"

"Twelve. He's some kind of genetic aberration. Some kind of saint."

She doesn't look at me while she talks. Her gaze is on the door: who comes in, how she might make her way out if I bore her. Her head is very erect, her neck long. She seems to be posing for the striking of a coin. I've spent my adult life among people superlatively aware of how the angle of light in a room illuminates their faces, who know the trick of drawing attention to themselves by withdrawing theirs from everyone else. Aviva had an instinct for these theatrical techniques. I wondered if she was more natural with her brother, forgot to arrange herself to be seen.

I ask her if she likes her roommate, and she shrugs. They barely speak, she tells me: different styles. I tell her it's the same with mine, a guy named David Yee. Typical Asian dork, I say, into his books all day. Me, except for crew season, I mostly hang out at the Dramat. That makes me a dork, too, I say, defiantly: let her think so. I tell her how it happened: how as a kid I wallowed in comic books and Dungeons & Dragons and a book of illustrated Greek myths I found in my fifth-grade classroom. When, prep year here at Auburn, we were assigned Aeschylus, I saw that it was all the same stuff: gore and rage and lamentations flying to the rafters. That was when I started to spend time in the theater. I dislike acting but I do everything else: lighting, construction, directing. This year I scored big—I'll be directing the Dramat's fall production of *Macbeth*.

We talk about our families. I tell her I'm from Jordan, New Jersey, half an hour from New York City. My father's a judge, my mother stays home. I'm not on good terms with my parents. My mother I don't mind so much: she's sad but harmless. My father I consider my enemy. "He's against everything that I am," I say. "Everything that makes me feel I can breathe."

This attracts her; she leans forward on her elbows, frowning anxiously. I see what I'd hoped to see: two swellings tipped toward the sticky table. Her breasts are widely spaced, with a deep shadowed tract of privacy between them.

"I might like having an enemy," she says. Her parents, she explains, permit everything, notice nothing.

I tell her about the first time I ever saw my father in the courthouse in Newark, sitting in his judicial robes. My mother had taken me along to do some shopping at Bamberger's; there were still a couple of decent stores in Newark in those days. My older brothers were in school. Maybe I was six, in kindergarten, with the half day off. I guess she thought she'd bring me by to see what my father did, what a significant man he was. I was frightened the moment I saw those black robes that swallowed him up and hid his hands. He was looking down at a man who spoke up at him, a man with a bald spot and no suit, just a regular pair of pants and a checkered shirt. My father interrupted the man sternly, rudely. In that moment I knew this man would be going to jail. He didn't know that yet, but I did. I could see him sweating and feel his fear. I could feel the pleasure my father took in making him listen. My father had a deceptively soft voice that made the listener strain to catch everything. The balding man, the stenographer, all the people in the court—they were leaning toward my father, afraid of missing something.

There are boys who tell girls things to evoke sympathy for themselves, or to convince a girl that they have feelings, they're sensitive. That's not my way, and it's not what I'm doing here. There's just something in this girl that makes me talky, unguarded, that makes me want to tell the truth.

"What about your mother?" she asks.

"She drinks."

Aviva's parents don't drink or yell. Her father is a surgeon, her mother a college professor. They don't hit or commit crimes. There's nothing you can actually pin on them, she says. She pushes disconsolately at the soupy remains of her ice cream. Her wrists are almost painfully slender; without the makeup and the breasts she could be fourteen. That's it, I decide. For years and years she was the skinny, shrimpy kid in the class, the bookish late bloomer. At sixteen she wakes up to find that she has tits, that her legs have grown shapely and long. What to do with these riches? She marvels at them in the mirror but her classmates still see the little girl, the teacher's pet. How can she show everyone the astonishing thing that has happened? After school she takes the bus downtown to Saks or Fields. She wanders the cosmetics department: counter after counter of lipsticks and blushes and perfumes and creams. It's like a palace: the lights, the super-reflected abundance. She has never worn makeup and has no idea where to begin. She drifts, touching the little tubes and bottles, and a young woman in a tight black suit croons to her: "Free makeup consultation . . . no obligation. Free makeup consultation . . . no obligation." Aviva turns, slowly, and the woman smiles. "Sit right here in this chair, darling. Such a pretty girl. Such lovely skin." One hundred and eighty-seven dollars: an hour later, that's what the bill comes to. Aviva pulls out the American Express card with her father's name on it, hands it over. Next she'll go upstairs and pick out sweaters, skirts, boots. Everything about her will be different now, sleek and sexy and soft to the touch. And every morning she'll go through the ritual the makeup lady taught her. The special soaps for cleaning, the dabbing on of foundation, the painstaking combing of mascara onto each lash. As Aviva steps on the escalator she feels heads turn toward her for the first time. She has become visible.

"Hello?" Aviva asks. For a moment there I wasn't gazing at her, wasn't absorbed in her, so busy was I with my tale. That shakes her, I can tell. Her confidence is so brittle. I won't tell her I was with another version of her; that would give her back her power. I like seeing her a little weak, a little uncertain.

She's waiting for me to say something. I reach across and touch her necklace, take the gold heart between my fingers, stroke it with my thumb. She grows still. Her eyes begin to blink more rapidly. I let the heart settle back on her chest, its tip pointing down toward the cleft between her breasts.

"Let's go," I say.

We walk toward the river, past the shingles on Nut Street—Rexall, Davis's Photo, Nick's Sporting Goods—and the fake Greek columns of the Guignol Theater. It's showing the movie *Alien*, which I already saw twice over the summer. Aviva stops at the window of the little chocolate shop; her gaze falls on a box containing truffles lined up like oversized nipples. I go straight inside and buy it for her. She is still laughing with surprise as I hand her the black box tied with a silver ribbon.

She opens the box. The six truffles inside cost many times more than I imagined they would. She puts a whole truffle into her mouth and holds out the box to me. Though I love sweets of every conceivable kind, I shake my head. I don't want to be distracted from this spectacle. And I am beginning to convince myself I truly like this girl. I can't help but enjoy the way she moves the truffle around in her mouth, sucking it, one cheek and then the other bulging out. It's vulgar; it's charming. She runs her tongue across the front of her teeth to remove the brown liquid that clings there.

I tell her I want to show her the Academy boathouse, and we walk down a grassy slope in that direction. I'm a coxswain in springtime, hunched in a narrow shell in my tight

Auburn T-shirt and my sun visor, master of the eight bodies lined up in front of me. They bend, lift, and bend to my command. I may look a little plump for a coxswain, but I don't actually weigh all that much—135 for my five feet six inches. I sweat off five of those pounds to make weight for the season. There in the shell my fluty voice doesn't bother me; it does what it needs to do, sends us skimming over the brownish water. We're a pretty good team. Last year our record was fourteen wins and four losses; my boat, third boat, placed second at the New England Championships.

I unlock the boathouse with a key I never returned at the end of last season. I like to come here alone sometimes to breathe in the smell of dust and damp canvas and spilled WD-40. Light sifts in through the high windows. There always seems to be a brackish odor too as if this shed perched on the ocean and not the river. The water outside is still and murky.

"What is crew, anyway?" Aviva asks. She isn't joking. She really doesn't know. They don't have it out in Chicago, she claims.

I explain the basics: eight boys in a shell, each with one oar, the sliding seats, the various calls. There's a skeg at the back of the shell, to help with direction. Sculling is different, doesn't have the coxswain, the rowers have an oar in each hand. It's maybe the oldest team sport in the world: a funerary inscription from 1400 BC, found in Egypt, mentions crew competitions. Crew races are held in *The Aeneid*.

Aviva's mind is wandering. I can see that she is someone who can't keep the slightest grip on things that don't interest her. I change tack and tell her how intimate it is in the shell, crammed tight in there, how when the frontmost rower strokes forward his face is right up against mine, his panting and my rhythmic shouting growing louder in unison, till we are skimming over the finish and I hear myself crying, in encouragement and triumph, "Oh, *yeah* . . . oh, *yeah*," how sometimes, when the race is over, the kid and I can't even look at each other, something so forceful has just passed between us.

She has been walking along touching the walls of the shed, an oar stand, an old rain poncho hanging from a hook, but now she turns, her mouth slightly parted. I can't bear it, her hair loose in the gloom, her saliva darkened with chocolate, the renewed heat of her attention. I move toward her, closing her in slowly as she continues her circuit—why has she turned away? Is she teasing me? I back her against the wall next to some shelves and, moving fast so I don't lose my nerve, yank her sweater around to get at her bra. I won't flee this time. In the thin light her bra shines out an odd bright purple color, the color of a grape lollipop. Joining the two cups is a rosette with an embroidered letter *P*. I see it all so clearly. The bra is snug; the lacy patterns in the cup are a signal that I am meant to continue.

She laughs quietly. "Hey, easy," she says. She puts her hands on my shoulders and leans in to kiss me slowly, but I have no patience and I mash my mouth against hers, working my tongue in. With one hand I reach behind her, jerking at her bra hook. She wriggles under me and tells me to stop it, to cool it, but I pay no attention, I'm too far gone. I feel my hardness against her softness. I've never gone all the way with a girl, but right now I need that in an entirely new fashion. Yes, I want to seize her, to fuck her, but something in me is also flying toward surrender. Is that hard to believe? Do my actions seem to contradict it? I assure you it was true. There's something in Aviva that calls out: *Drown*. Everything that is solid about me is meant to sink inside her and dissolve; my mouth wants to be sealed and my eyes sewn shut. I want not to know myself anymore. Not to be this squat, impotent body, this restless, angry mind. And there are so many obstacles to get past, so many real, hard, solid things. Her breasts—I am wrenching them out of her bra and squeezing them; what to do about them? Her sweater, nauseatingly hairy, the tangle of her necklaces . . . I am frantically trying to manage all this when I become aware that Aviva is seriously fighting me. She is pushing back against me and shouting, trying to duck under my arms. I'm startled but unbelieving and press her even closer to the wall, pinning her mouth with mine: surely she needs me just as I need her. This is all supposed to be.

She puts her palm against my chin and gives me a hard shove, backing me away long enough that I can see her face, the unmistakable rage that is there. Long enough to make me wonder what the hell I am doing. Aviva steps away from the wall and stares at me, breathing hard.

"You motherfucker," she says. "You fucking motherfucker."

I move toward her again, slowly this time, trying to show her I mean to be different, to be careful, and she flinches and raises her fists. She is tiny: five feet tall and delicate-boned, but if I continue I will find teeth, muscles.

"You touch me and I will report you," she says. "I will get the entire disciplinary system to come down on you. I will . . ." I watch the strength rise up in her, light her up.

"You come on and try me," she says. "Come on. Come on."

I can't move. She holds my eyes as she pushes herself back into her bra, her sweater, sidling along to the barnlike door before deliberately turning her back on me, daring me to interfere, and wrenching it open. The light smacks my eyes and by the time I make Aviva out again she is half-way up the hill. She takes small steps, transparent in her desire not to seem to be hurrying. Her hand reaches up and smooths back her hair.

I have never heard a girl say the words *disciplinary system* before.

At that time I am used to thinking I have more than one chance at things, many chances, in fact. I do poorly in prep biology, but my transcript is revised after I attend summer school. I crack up my father's car, but the insurance company pays out, and my driver's license is reinstated. Over and over again my parents convince themselves that my bad study habits, slovenliness, deep pessimism, and lack of ambition will undergo a change. And I believe too that when the moment is right, when I want it enough, I will in fact succeed as a student, son, lover, and friend. This time, for the first time—though not the last—I know I've truly blown something. I don't know how I know. It's an unfamiliar feeling.

7

That Saturday I hang lights for the dance in the Student Center before meeting my girlfriend, Lisa, who wants to go out to a movie. The Saturday Night Committee usually gets the Dramat to help out with setup. I never stay for the dances themselves, so I don't see Aviva and Seung together, swaying under the lights I've put up, pressing themselves close for the very first time. "Wild Horses," by the Stones—they would have danced to that. What else would there have been? "Money," by the Flying Lizards. "Oh, Atlanta." "Refugee." "Rock Lobster." The beat is jumpy and strong, and Aviva can't stop herself; she has to move. She keeps Seung out on the floor for every song; in the short breaks between sets they plunge into the night air and wipe their wet faces with their sleeves. The rambunctious, cynical music streams through her, makes her laugh aloud. She's never happier than when she's dancing. Even her makeup can flake and rub away; she still believes she's there.

8

Carlyle moans in her sleep. Her short nightgown is up above her knees. Her legs are open, quivering; her breath is quick and shallow. Aviva looks up from her math homework. She is writing by the light of a table lamp set on the floor. She likes to work late into the night and regularly she stays in her friends' room after they have gone to bed. They don't mind. Carlyle and Lena ask Aviva to report on everything they do and say while they're unconscious, because both are incorrigible sleep talkers and sleepwalkers. Once, Carlyle walked straight out of the dorm and Aviva found her playing hopscotch on the blacktop out back, her eyes glassy, mumbling about winning a ribbon. Earlier tonight, dreaming, Lena called out: "You play piano so well! Don't cry, don't cry."

What is happening now, Aviva will not report. Carlyle's eyes move rapidly beneath the lids. Aviva watches her,

fascinated. Carlyle knows, she thinks. She knows the pleasure that Aviva wants to know. Not the kind that comes from
touching yourself but the other kind, the kind that involves
the man on you and inside you. Carlyle's legs jerk hard several times, and then, finally, she passes back into silence.

Aviva gathers her books and papers and leaves the room.
She never goes to her own room until she is so tired she
knows she will fall quickly to sleep. It is 11:00 PM and she
is not tired. She finds the pay phone, an upright coffin with
a clouded glass door that smells of BO, petrified chewing
gum, old, sour wood. Names of long-ago students, all male,
are carved in the frame.

The phone rings six, seven, eight times. Marshall picks up.

"It's ten o'clock there. You should be in bed," Aviva tells
him.

"I *was* in bed. I got out to answer. I knew it was going to
be you."

"You did not."

"I did. I always know."

"Angel face."

She can see the face he makes, not angelic.

"Are you doing well in school?" she asks.

"Um."

"Marshall. You don't want to have to go to summer
school again."

"I know," he says sadly. "I want to do summer baseball."

"So do yourself a favor."

"We'll see. Do you like it there?"

"I love it."

"Good. Do you have a boyfriend?"

"Yes. Next question?"

"Do you want Dad?"

"I guess so. Yes."

A short silence. "If he doesn't tell you something interesting, ask for me again," Marshall tells her. She can hear the creak of the old floors as he walks away. She can picture him perfectly. He wears cotton pajama pants with a faded Cubs T-shirt on top. He still looks like a little boy, with a little boy's round face and soft feet.

"Hello," her father says. He speaks to her the same way he speaks to his patients, clearing his throat first.

"I just wanted to say hi." Despair moves inside of her. Why did she think it would make her feel better to call home? How many times does she need to make this same mistake?

"Well, hi."

"Is everything all right with Marshall?"

"Well, I think so."

"Where's Mom?" Stupid question.

"I really don't know."

Aviva begins to talk quickly, hardly knowing what she is saying. "I've been invited to my friend Lena's for Thanksgiving. She lives in Philadelphia. I went to a play here last night, *The Chairs*. You know, by Ionesco." Silence—either her father hasn't heard of Ionesco or he has nothing to say about him. She asks him if he can send money for the train fare to Philadelphia. "Is everything okay there?"

He breathes in and out, that familiar labored breath. "Well, your mother is a very, very difficult person," he answers.

"I know."

She almost forgets to ask to speak to Marshall again. "What?" she begs. "He didn't say anything."

"They're finally splitting up," Marshall tells her. "Mom moved out for a few days so Dad could get his things together and find an apartment. Then she'll come back and he'll go. I'll stay right here, in my room and everything."

"Why didn't you call me?" she cries.

"I did. This girl went to look for you and said you weren't there. She said she'd give you the message."

"Jesus H. Christ. I never got it. Who did you talk to?"

"I don't remember."

"You do remember."

"Well, I won't tell you, you'll just get angry at her. Do you think it's going to be a good thing or a bad thing?"

"I don't know," Aviva says. "They both hate being alone." She's quiet a moment. "I bet it won't take long for Dad to disappear." Suddenly she is very afraid. "Oh, God, what if he stops paying my tuition?"

9

We claimed to despise Auburn, its endless restrictions, its earnest propaganda of order. We disobeyed the rules, called Auburn a prison. But the truth was—and we knew it—Auburn was freer than any place we'd ever been. There were no parents here and little supervision. The eyes watching us, when they watched, did so without the jealousies and fears and hopes of our families. In this radical garden we could reinvent ourselves; we could seed the adults we would become. *Gnaritas et Patientia* read our school motto— Knowledge and Patience—but the knowledge we wanted was knowledge of the body: how to enlarge it through pleasure and how to make it disappear. Sex would yank us into adulthood; drugs would dissolve our dumb physical limits. Infinitude of the mind and the body. Somewhere God (the principal, the dean of students, our dorm heads) walked at a distance, allowing us our experiments, our discoveries. The worst thing that could possibly happen to any of us, we knew, was to be brought home, shipped back to childhood.

10

They are still quite new at this, but they know what to do. They put it together out of what they've read in books and seen in magazines, out of dreams, instinct, in imitation of the others, the very few, they've been with. Her lips are always soft, barely parted at first. This excites him deeply, the patience she insists upon, the way she opens to him only slowly. She sets their rhythm, yields a little, then a little more, and once she is open and gaping, she exacts submission from him in return, plunging into his mouth, licking roughly. Then she is tender and soft again. She leads, then she lets him lead. They are young, they can kiss and press against each other for hours, gradually twisting out of their clothing. For other acts there is plenty of time, all the time in the world.

Where can they go for privacy, for these hours of leisurely pleasure? There are the woods beyond the gymnasium: clearings with crushed soda cans and used condoms, and, if you know how to get there, the Bog, although often

the tree-ringed lake known by that name is populated with
students getting wasted on the muddy banks. There is her
room or his room on a Saturday night. Parietals are from
8:00 to 10:00 PM, with the lights on and the door open a
minimum of two inches. Many of the faculty members on
duty never come upstairs to check. If they do, one can gam-
ble on technical compliance and a cheeky argument ("We
thought the desk lamp counted!"—when the overhead light
is off and a tall stack of books blocks the lamp's glow).

There's the bank of the river where it dwindles to a creek
as it passes through the woods and there are the alleys on
Nut Street and there's the Guignol Theater in the darkness.
There are the music building's practice rooms, whose doors
have a window that can be blocked by a record album cover.
Faculty members—some of them, anyway—pretend they
don't see. There is plenty of opportunity.

Seung lays his head on her breasts. He traces the deep
indentation of her waist. "W-O-M-A-N," he spells out, drawing the letters along the swell of her hip. "That curve spells
Woman." She laughs. Three months ago, even three weeks
ago, she was still only a girl.

The gray light of late afternoon washes the floor and the
bed. Sunday, Seung's room. Seung spent the hour before
their meeting on the case of a prep whose homesickness has
not let up, who is desperate to leave school. "I'm not cut out
for this place," the boy keeps saying. He cries at night, and
then cries some more when he remembers that his roommate will tell everyone else about the crying. Seung called

in the roommate and told him that this kind of ratting-out wouldn't be tolerated. "Be a man; show some compassion," Seung said. He thinks he may have gotten through to the kid, and the homesick one has agreed to give school another week. They'll talk again next Sunday.

"You're a good proctor, a good model," Aviva says, splaying her hand to look at it against Seung's strong thigh. Her white skin, his olive skin.

"Maybe," Seung says. "The kids know I break more rules than they do."

"So long as the faculty don't know."

"They know. Everyone knows. I've never been able to be all good, baby. I'm just very good at *looking* good—and not getting caught. There's an unspoken deal: as long as I'm not obvious, the Powers let it go by." He bends and kisses the curve he so likes. "Anyway, something like you can't be truly against the rules."

"Don't be silly."

"I'm not silly."

A cool draft flows in through the old, misaligned windows. The desks hold handwritten essays and class books: Jonathan Kozol, *Marxism and Society*, *Die Leiden des jungen Werthers*. Sterne has agreed not to return until seven o'clock. They smuggled Aviva up here, shameless. Aviva waited in the Weld entranceway, chatting with Sterne, looking like someone who had just dropped by to say hi. Detweiler stood sentry on the second floor and Giddings, Detweiler's roommate, on the third. They made sure no one was moving in the corridors, then signaled down. It was easy—ten seconds and Aviva was inside Seung's room. Seung jammed the door lock with chewing gum, just in case Mr. Glass, the dorm head, hears suspicious movement and attempts an entrance with his skeleton key. Aviva would have time to crawl under the heap of coats in the corner. So Seung says.

A late October pre-dusk silence, broken occasionally by a shout outside the window. Aviva lays herself out to Seung's touch. His fingers move slowly, sounding her. His fingers are sentient; they study and anticipate. Her veins flood. She was made for this. Seung turns her onto her belly, pushing her hair to one side, and presses his thumbs hard into the muscles along her spine and ringing her neck, bunched at her shoulders. She feels herself being put together by him piece by piece.

They are young, don't forget this. Seung imagines what it would be like to be inside her, but it's like imagining a field on the other side of a distant fence. It is a place it will take time to get to, somewhere he will gain eventually but cannot see distinctly now.

She is less curious about exploring his body, or in any case less forthright. To touch pleases her less than to be touched. Seung's hairless chest, though broad and strong, is tender-looking, like paper that might tear under her fingers. The swelling between his legs she will cup and kiss if it is masked by the stiff fabric of his jeans, but when it is released, she finds it menacing and is afraid to handle it.

There is something raw and unfinished about the thing; its asymmetry bothers her, as does the massive gelatinous sack of balls. She loses confidence when she sees his penis; she sees herself being overpowered, forced. Nothing frightens her more. Her girlfriends back home had a game. If you had to choose, would you rather be raped or murdered? Murdered, she always answered.

She climbs on top of Seung, straddles him, bends down to kiss him deeply, then straightens and withholds herself from him. He reaches up and makes a breastplate for her with his palms. She stretches out next to him full-length. He kisses her neck, shoulders, hips. He trembles with the effort it takes to be gentle. When they go to the woods, hands up under each other's sweaters, their corduroys unzipped, his briefs fill again and again with sticky ejaculate. She closes her eyes when they kiss. He watches her, always. They go on and on, then rest without talking. They daydream for a long time, and then one or the other begins the touching again. The afternoon is endless. No one will come to bother them, no one will knock on the door.

Seung falls asleep with his cheek on her naked belly. Aviva listens to his quiet snoring for a while, then falls asleep too.

11

Even the teachers talked about them. Seung Jung and Aviva
Rossner were bewitched. Their hands moved over each other as they reluctantly separated at classroom doors. They
stood kissing while streams of students passed around
them. There were plenty of couples on campus about whom
it was understood that they did all the things that married
couples do, but the etiquette to which they adhered, always,
was dissimulation. In public they were dignified, clean. You
heard it said, at times, that Aviva didn't know any better because she was a Jew—vulgar, totally unschooled in Yankee
discretion. And she led Seung. So we sneered, we criticized.
We even made comments about mongrel relationships,
Oriental and white. But secretly we were delighted and in-
flamed. Most of us probably simply enjoyed imagining various acts, various permissions, but I know now that there
was something more urgent in my own recreations of what

went on between Aviva and her lover. I didn't just imagine them *doing things*. I imagined a kind of fire that flew up around them and consumed them. It sounds laughably dramatic, but don't underestimate the metaphysical yearnings of a seventeen-year-old. That's the secret of teenage sex, I think. For none of us was it really about asses and crotches, sucking cock or licking pussy. It's adults who so often think in those terms, with such a lack of imagination. We beginners experienced sex as psyche more than body, as vulnerability and power, exposure and flight, being anointed, saved, transfigured. To fail at it—to *do it wrong*—was to experience (and please do not smirk; try to remember what it was like, once upon a time) the death of one's ideal soul.

12

The bus to Boston leaves after the end of Saturday classes and returns at seven. Aviva makes the trip with Lena and Carlyle, who sit together. Aviva has the opposite bench to herself. She opens her novel: Hardy's *Tess of the d'Urbervilles*. The bus sends its vibrations through the vinyl banquette seats and into her thighs. She tenses experimentally, shifts position. Her jeans tighten against her crotch and she feels herself contract to a sharp, sparking point. Turning a page without reading it, she daydreams: a boy, not Seung, tracing circles with his finger around her cunt, which is open, exposed, afraid. The boy is faceless: blond curls, strong hands. A tongue licks the open space. Her breasts hum against the dense cloth of her oxford blouse. It is so simple just to tighten gently inside the way she does when she wants to hold back her pee, channeling the shuddering of the moving bus. A man—the boy is gone—places her on all fours, shoves his stiffness in and out of her. She is whole once again, a delicious liquor spreads into her arms. In the bus seat she moves not at all, no one could possibly tell what she is making happen. She turns another page, for show. At the end, when the deep cramping pleasure comes, she pretends to stretch—Ah, doesn't reading on a bus make one feel tired and restless!

Carlyle knows how to get to the bottle shop near South Station that will sell to underage kids. She did it all the time last year, she says, it's a snap. The best thing to get is Bacardi 151—the most bang per swallow. Lena and Aviva wait across the street. Like Aviva, Lena is new this year and learning the way things are done. The building next to the bottle shop has no windows, no front door. The steps are strewn with trash. The girls carry the flat bottle in a paper bag, pass it hand to hand as they look for the subway. Aviva's perfume is called Opium; Carlyle's is something floral and sweeter. Lena wears neither perfume nor makeup. She has rather crooked features and glasses, but Aviva admires her breasts, which are ample and high, and her elegant legs. She's of Greek stock, with a beautiful last name, Joannou. Carlyle is a different breed entirely, Virginian, with thick blond hair and generous hips and a big white Southern smile.

"There are countries you can't even sell this stuff in," Carlyle tells them. She heard it from the guy behind the counter. He was flirting with her. Grown men frequently flirt with her.

"Which ones?" asks Lena.

"He didn't say."

Aviva sips, waits a few minutes to see what the effect is, asks for the bottle again. Have I said that she is a girl who fears what is inside of her? She wants to be giddy and silly, self-forgetful, a state she has not experienced since she was perhaps nine or ten years old. At the same time she does not want to say something that cannot be unsaid, or do something that will be hard to forget. She does not want to fall down or vomit, make a fool of herself.

Her head stays cool and clear. She drinks more.

On Beacon Hill the girls go into a little shop with bright scarves and hats on ornate racks. Lena and Carlyle don't have enough money to buy anything. The items aren't to Carlyle's taste anyway. She prefers traditional and tailored things: turtlenecks, sturdy blazers, argyle socks. Aviva winds a purple mohair scarf around her neck. She adds a dark fedora with a stiff purple feather stuck in the crown, pulling it down low, shading her eyes.

The others are delighted. "Get it, get it," they urge her.

Aviva pays for the hat with her father's credit card. He has yet to cancel all the accounts. That will happen later, when he wants to make sure her mother cannot spend any more of his money. The lovely scarf she unwinds and returns to the rack. She can't have everything. She allows herself extravagances by denying herself other extravagances. The equation convinces her she is temperate. The hat costs seventy dollars. On the street her limbs tingle, she breathes and speaks rapidly, excited by her purchase. She grabs the rum for another gulp. It's time for something to eat, she cries. She is growing warm under her peacoat.

"You look like a gorgeous gangster," says Lena.

They go to Faneuil Hall, drawn past the stalls of jewelry and pottery to the smell of something hot and fried. A stout woman is patting out large disks of dough and dropping them into a vat of rippling oil. The dough is retrieved, drained on paper towels, heaped with powdered sugar. The girls each have one.

It's delicious: the flaky, oily bread, the sugar turning into a sweet paste in the mouth. The paper towel each has been given as a napkin becomes soaked, filthy. The girls buy peanuts and pour their rum into cans of 7-Up.

Near the exit they pause before a Häagen-Dazs stall. Carlyle says she can't, not after the fried dough. She absolutely must lose ten pounds. Lena is out of cash. Aviva hesitates while passing the money for both of them over the counter. What is this hesitation? Two scoops with generous skirts perch atop two browned cones. The stall smells richly of cream and toasted sugar. Chunks of chocolate stud the ice cream like showy jewels. Something grips Aviva, whispers that she's gone too far. One cone is passed into Lena's hand, already dripping from the crown. Aviva accepts the other as if hypnotized. The transaction has been concluded: she will have to eat it now. The first bite is so delicious she closes her eyes. She sucks on the chunks of chocolate that remain in her mouth after the sweet cream dissolves.

She takes another bite, and another, impatient to repeat the pleasure. She waits to feel sated, sick of it, for the pleasure to diminish, but it does not. She eats faster as if she might be able to overrun the pleasure and leave it behind. With a sudden spastic motion she flings the half-eaten cone into a garbage bin. Relief floods her.

"I would have taken that!" cries Lena.

Aviva is safe now. Her fright has passed. She reaches up and strokes the feather on her hat. It is all right.

At South Station they take some last nips from the bottle before shoving it into the pocket of Lena's down vest. "Are you drunk?" they ask each other. Carlyle smiles, nodding. Lena hums to herself, swaying from side to side. Her fingers start to play *Rhapsody in Blue*. Whenever she is happy or high, she moves them to the notes of Gershwin.

"I don't feel anything," complains Aviva.

"You're too careful, baby," Carlyle tells her.

13

Early November, flat skies, weak light, early nights. The dormitories are cold. In Aviva's mailbox Monday is a letter asking her to come see the dean of students.

The dean asks if Miss Rossner knows why she has been called in. She does not.

"Saturday's dance . . ." he explains.

It was a dance sponsored by the Afro-Am society, heavy on the disco. Aviva isn't fond of the sound or the beat but she and Seung never miss an opportunity to dance. Before heading over to the Student Center, Aviva drank tequila from a bottle Seung keeps in one of his winter boots. She let long streams course into her mouth. She and Seung kissed on the dance floor for a long time, pressing into each other. After a while they left the Student Center and walked toward the sports fields, stopping behind the tennis courts. They lay down, throwing off their coats and unbuttoning their shirts. These are the things that Aviva remembers. She does not remember the crowd on the dance floor falling back to watch the two of them, their mouths and their hands. She does not know that a knot of students followed them out to the tennis courts to spy from a distance. Dean Ruwart has to tell her about that.

Aviva frowns, folds her arms, looks down. This foolish man, with his close-cropped hair, his babyish cheeks, behaving as if she has done something wrong. Shame and fear rise up in her, but it is the shame of having been seen without knowing it and the fear of becoming not the mysterious object of boys' desire but a punch line in their dirty jokes. As for what she and Seung were actually doing—she refuses the idea that she has anything to apologize for. Has she cheated on a test? Has she stolen something from the science lab? Sex is natural, sex is her birthright, the pursuit that has at long last arrived to make sense of her world.

The dean tells her that the two of them are being put on restrictions. Restrictions means checking in to their dorms at 8:00 PM, same as the preps and the lowers, even on Saturday nights. The normal check-in hour for uppers is 9:00 PM, for seniors, 10:00 PM. Another violation of school decorum during this time will mean probation. Beyond probation, Dean Ruwart doesn't need to add, looms expulsion. Does she understand why this action is being taken?

"No," she says.

She tells a friend or two about the encounter, how she said "no" to the dean and he merely shook his head and let her go. It becomes a little story going around: Aviva stood up to old Ruwart, wouldn't be cowed. Didn't apologize. But for a long time Aviva is secretly mortified by the image of all those bodies forming a circle around her and Seung on the dance floor, ogling them in the dark, the lights strobing on and off their damp, drunken faces. Then all those eyes watching for a flash of breast in the grass.

Restrictions does not make as much difference as it might. She and Seung can still sit in the common room after dinner and nuzzle, take afternoon walks in the woods. On Saturdays they hide in the bathroom of the library while the building is locked up at six, and then have the entire place to themselves, the wide concrete stairwells, the airy stacks. They watch the sky darken, holding hands. They kneel, kissing, in the 900s—books on Morocco and Tunisia and Algeria—while the heat in the building clanks off and the temperature slowly drops. At ten minutes to eight they watch for passersby and then stroll out of the building: first Aviva, then Seung. The door isn't alarmed, Seung tells her, and she wonders how he knows the things he knows. When has he been here before, and with whom?

When the month is over they celebrate with a movie at the Guignol: *All That Jazz*, with Ann Reinking in fishnet stockings and a bowler hat, sardonic Roy Scheider, Jessica Lange as Death with a white veil and porcelain skin. Aviva would like to be all of them: Reinking, Scheider, Lange, even the little girl—the Roy Scheider character's daughter—in pigtails and a leotard, who wraps her legs around him, clinging, when her visit with him is over. She would like to move the way Reinking does; she would like to dance out her life in a succession of musical numbers: the sexy number, the sad number, the enraged number, the pleading number, the celebratory number, the death number.

Later that night, Carlyle tells Aviva that when the preps and lowers were checking in, their dorm head, Señora Ivarra, looked at her chart and said, "Ah, the very sociable young lady is once again allowed to stay out."

"She said that? In front of everybody?"

"Only the ones in front probably heard. I came in early because Gene had a headache. A lot of the teachers don't like you, Aviva. You should be careful. They can make trouble for you. I've been here longer than you, so I know. I'm not saying don't live your life. Just be smart about things, okay?"

Aviva is surprised to find her feelings quite hurt. Teachers not liking her? Why shouldn't they like her? They've always liked her before! She's a good student. She participates in class. Perhaps Carlyle exaggerates. But in any case, what is there to worry about? She got the message—there are forces out there that will rein her and Seung in—and she'll be toeing the line from now on. Just enough.

14

Over the years I've come to understand that telling someone's story—telling it, I mean, with a purity of intention, in an attempt to get at that person's real desires and sufferings—is at one and the same time an act of devotion and an expression of sadism. *You* are the one moving the bodies around, putting words in their mouths, making them do what you need them to do. You insist, they submit.

I didn't give up the theater when I left Auburn. It claimed me for good. I moved from managing the bodies in my boat, shouting at them to *move your asses to your heels*, to *put your blood and piss into it*, to the supposedly more genteel managements of the stage. In college I made theater my major, against my father's wishes, and afterward got an MFA at Yale. Since then I've worked as a director at various small companies in New York City and regionally. You won't have heard of me; I'm just one of the many who toil on the subfloors of art, telling ourselves our time will come . . .

After Seung's death, after graduation, I learned some things from Carlyle. She and Lena were putting together a memory book about Seung for Aviva. They hoped to fill it with anecdotes from anyone they could find with a connection to Seung: fellow students, teachers, old buddies from Jordan. Anyone from his year in Weld. Carlyle and I ended up staying on the phone for a long time. Grief—or the imputation of grief—knocks down barriers between people. Carlyle had been collecting the pictures Seung used to draw and give to people—did I have one? One of those drawings with all the intricate cross-hatching that he made with those thin-tipped pens? I didn't.

I steered the conversation to Aviva. Asked the predictable questions: How was she holding up? etc. Our exchange then took an unexpected turn. Carlyle was talkative, even indiscreet. Aviva was never destined to be happy, she claimed. Even before what happened to Seung. She had always been tightly wound and afraid. Afraid of what? Of so many things. Of sweets and booze, of losing control. Carlyle used to catch Aviva looking in mirrors, coming close and then standing back again, over and over, as if she couldn't quite make herself appear. Seung was good for her, pushed her to be more adventurous, to loosen up a bit. Of course, sometimes dicey things happened. Seung was, you could say, a little too enthusiastic about his drugs. And there was that time the two of them got caught in a hotel stairwell in New York, practically got arrested . . .

15

Certain nights, Lena cries, saying that she's afraid of dying a virgin. Aviva and Carlyle stay up talking to her, reassuring her that she will find a boyfriend someday, that she will be loved. Privately they are not so generous: Lena is not pretty. Perhaps she never will find a boyfriend. They are glad they are not Lena, with her nervous gestures and hopeless crushes and anxieties. They can't foresee that Lena, by her twenties, will have more lovers, and more pleasures, than both of them put together.

It's been a bad week for Lena. Her aunt phoned to say that her mother had had another breakdown and was back in the hospital.

"I'm sorry about Thanksgiving," Lena tells Aviva. Her aunt already has more people coming than she can handle.

"Stop it. How can you be sorry? Anyway, Seung wants me to go home with him. He's going to ask his parents about it."

"What if they say no?"

"I can always stay in the dorm."

Carlyle says, "Don't *ever* do that. It's the saddest thing in the world. You have Thanksgiving dinner with the faculty who stay, and in the afternoon you have to sing at the Portsmouth soup kitchen."

"I can't sing," says Aviva.

"It doesn't matter."

Carlyle's boyfriend is Gene Murchie, a senior, large, shaggy-haired, abrupt. He and Carlyle have been seeing each other for over a year; during the summer, while they were parted, he grew a mustache. He plays varsity lacrosse and wants to be a sculptor. In warm weather he strips off his shirt at any opportunity to allow the other boys to observe and envy his perfect pecs. He flies into rages, claiming that Carlyle flirts with his friends, that she steals money from him, that she has written letters to his teachers slandering him, in an attempt to lower his grades. This is why, he says, he will end up at University of Vermont instead of Stanford. He is crazy and nobody seems to know it or do anything about it. He has hit Carlyle more than once. For days she sobs and talks about killing herself, and then she reports that their love has never been stronger, all the hard times are finished and behind them.

Carlyle smokes Pall Malls, Lena clove cigarettes imported from Indonesia, Aviva the lowest-tar brand she can find, usually Carltons. She is thinking of quitting; she's afraid of what smoking is doing to her insides, and sometimes she cheats on the inhaling. Lena can do smoke rings, and rings within rings. There are other regulars in the butt room:

Kelly Finch and Dorota Noel, who has a single on the third floor. Dorota is from London. She has a barking laugh and likes to command the conversation. Aviva grows silent in the basement room filled with torn and stained furniture, the refuge of decades of Auburn's would-be rebels. She does not love Seung the way Carlyle loves Gene; she cannot find within herself that self-abasement. She does not nurture obsessions like Lena or go on adventures like Dorota. She fears that if she speaks, her feelings will be found wanting.

Seung's room is sunny and smells of fresh laundry. He puts Jean-Pierre Rampal on the turntable. He and Aviva kneel on the bed, moving their hands over skin, taking off their clothing piece by piece. Three hours of kissing is nothing to them. Nothing else calls them. The sun falls in the sky. They doze and wake. Again Seung touches Aviva into being: she is here, large, alive. Her good fortune is immense. Seung still cannot get over the deep hourglass of her body: the strenuous indentation at her waist and then the wide flare of the hips. The breasts spread out like huge coins. They are on the floor; she asks him to come inside her. More and more she wants to be done with this thing, this virginity, that keeps her from the ultimate pleasure, knowledge, and power.

Seung rocks back on his heels, hesitating. It can't be so simple: just to be asked, just to do it. He's frightened: *What if* . . . He doesn't know what the *what if* is. Something dark flies up in front of his vision. He didn't think that Aviva, even with all her forthrightness, would ask for this so

matter-of-factly, and so soon. He thought the prerogative
to ask would be his.

Please, she says. She smiles.

He takes her face in his hands, happy now too, kissing
her exuberantly, resting his forehead briefly against hers.

"I have condoms," she whispers. She's had them since
Chicago, got them at a drugstore in a neighborhood not her
own, looked the older woman behind the counter straight
in the eye. She would be ready when the opportunity came.
She doesn't want to be stupid. She knows a girl has to take
care of herself.

Seung tears open the foil package. Aviva's already opened
a couple in her stash, to see what they look like and how
they work. She likes the smell of the slippery, flesh-colored
coil, an industrial smell that reminds her of certain plastic playthings she had when she was little. Seung turns the
condom over in his hands, studies it with that engineer's
brain of his, as if figuring out how it was manufactured.
Then he places it over the head of his penis and worries
it down. Aviva drops her eyes; the sight is too stark. She
lies back, supporting her head with one arm so as not to
feel so stiff and defenseless. Seung stretches out on top of
her as she parts her legs uncertainly. He moves himself
around, shifting and poking as if he can't quite locate her.
It doesn't occur to her to reach down and help him. In the
dirty books she's read, and in her fantasies, the man enters,
that's all there is to it. Seung pushes; the moment is here at
last. She reaches up to clasp his shoulders. *It's happening,*

she thinks. She's going to dissolve now, to expand. She is going to know, completely, how to live. The sensation of pressure recedes; Seung is not there after all. She feels him move against her a few more times and is puzzled. Finally, to change the rhythm, she struggles up to a sitting position and embraces him.

Wrapped around each other they kiss deeply. She could spend all afternoon with her mouth softly open against his, the press of his lips making her aware of every nerve in her own. She feels him harden once more against her thigh. He cups her cunt, holds his hand there, like he's weighing her. She sighs. He rolls her onto her back and approaches again. The moment the tip of his cock touches the thatch of curly hair something pulls back in him again; he shrivels internally and then externally. He cannot believe what is happening. His heart grows hot with desire and anger. He does not understand. He pitches himself against her, butting against her cunt, clumsy as he never is clumsy. She stirs uneasily beneath him. Her buttocks ache; there's a pain in her side and she wriggles to relieve the pressure. Seung begins to pant, not with arousal but with frustration, with grim intent. Aviva feels like a thing beneath him, an object he wants to conquer. "Stop," she says. "Just stop." She sits up. Her open legs shame and grieve her. She closes them. Then she begins to cry.

Dorota is giving them the latest installment on Marvin Geohagen. Marvin Geohagen weighs 280 pounds. He is a shot-putter; his hands are the size of catcher's mitts. He is one of those athletes, boys almost exclusively, who come to

Auburn after they've already graduated from high school. They are most of them not that bright, but passing grades in senior-year courses and continued athletic prowess mean they might make it into Notre Dame or even Dartmouth. They sit together at one table in the dining hall, razz each other in their deep voices, and ogle the girls who have obvious breasts. They can't have any of them and they know it, not for real; the girls all think they're too good for these meatheads.

Last week Marvin Geohagen asked Dorota to take a walk with him. They went far out into the woods. I want you to be my girlfriend, he said.

Suddenly she found herself on her knees, his enormous hands gripping her head. "What was I supposed to do?" Dorota asks. She blows a stream of smoke toward the mold-stained ceiling.

The upshot is that Marvin is in love with her now. He follows her out of the dining hall, waits for her outside of her classes. They must be together, he says; she is the love of his life. She's told him that they're not right for each other ("because you're a bloody oaf, Marvin"—that's what she *should* have said); she has invented a serious boyfriend back in England. He can't hear a thing. Today, finally, she told him she didn't love him. That, in fact, he repulsed her.

"He said, 'You cunt. I'm going to hurt you.' And then he walked away." Dorota pauses, then screeches with laughter.

Aviva cries on Seung's bed, on and on, the way she hasn't cried since she was a child, her sobs deep and shuddering, involuntary gasps seizing her like hiccups. She hides her face. The shock is the confirmation that she cannot be loved. She wails, pounds the mattress. She has been expecting the proof for years, expecting to be blindsided by it even as she hoped to deceive and evade it. And here it is. He cannot enter her. Something in her repels him. She knew it, she knew it. Seung believes that he wants her, but his body tells the truth. She puts her nails to her face, pulls at her hair, but even this kind of abandonment she is incapable of: she does not want to scar herself. Even in despair she is self-protecting.

Seung holds her. The shame is his own; he can't understand why she carries on so. He's failed. It is the feeling most familiar to him. That sinking down, that scrabbling in the dirt, never finding purchase. The taste of boots and gravel. He had a dog once, never healthy. In a moment of weakness his father bought it at a county fair. It used to vomit on the living room rug until his father insisted it be put down. Before that could happen the addled animal wandered into the road and got hit by a car. A bone, clean as a bone on a dinner plate, stuck out of the dog's leg at the knee. Seung's mother drove Seung and his brother and the shrieking dog to the vet, who gave it a shot that took away both pain and life. Seung remembers the feeling of total failure: the failure to comfort, the failure to preserve life, the failure to be a normal American boy with a normal American dog that romped and played and fetched sticks.

Dorota lights another cigarette. She smokes all the time, even in her room, spraying her perfume around afterward.

When Aviva wears Dorota's sweaters they smell like smoke and Chanel No. 5. They hang long on Aviva, like men's sweaters; she rolls and rolls the sleeves.

"I think you should tell someone about Marvin," Aviva says. "I mean, report him."

The others look at her in amazement.

The light is fading from Seung's window. Aviva is talking. Words spill out of her, endless. All of her usual grace and self-control are undone: her face is swollen, her voice shrill. She frightens Seung. *You don't love me, I'm a monster, you don't really love me, I knew this would happen, do you feel like I don't love you?, you don't love me.*

"Oh, God," he pleads.

They fall asleep, exhausted, holding hands.

"Seung, Seung." She shakes him. "There's someone at the door."

Someone is tapping quietly, repeatedly, trying to signal. Seung throws on a shirt and cracks the door.

"It's a quarter to nine," Sterne tells him. "Man, you've got to get her out of here."

16

Years later, Aviva will surely know that it happens so often
it's almost comical: the man wilting at that first approach.
A woman is always frightening the first time. Years from
now, when a man fails, perhaps she will hold him and tell
him it's all right, it doesn't matter, there's no rush . . . And
later, things *will* be all right, and he will forget all about that
initial humiliation, his fears, his stumble.

Maybe events would have unfolded as they did even if
Aviva hadn't wept and carried on that evening in Seung's
room. Maybe Seung believed, deep down, that if he pos-
sessed her, she would grow tired of him and move on to one
of the many boys who would have been glad to capture her.
Maybe he sensed that he could hold on to her longer by deferring her satisfaction. Or maybe, with his extraordinary
instinct, he intuited that intercourse would not be satisfaction for her, that for her the peak had already been reached.

To enter her body would unsettle and eventually anger her. He was protecting Aviva from herself, then? Obviously I can't know that for sure.

17

Dak-ho Jung reads both the *New York Times* and the paper from Seoul each day: the news sections, the business sections, the obituaries. The Seoul paper arrives ten days late, so he reads that first. Then he turns to the *Times*. He sits for an hour or more, Wagner playing on the turntable. When his coffee cup grows empty he holds it out, his arm appearing from behind the big vertical sheets. His wife, trained as a doctor in Korea, comes instantly to replenish his drink.

They clasp Aviva's hand warmly, both of them, but Seung has told her that they will never accept her: they will smile, heap food on her plate, exhaust themselves in errands to make her comfortable, yet they will hate her in their hearts.

Seung's brother, Chaz (given name Chin-hua), is also home for Thanksgiving. He goes to Cornell. There he started an organization called Friends of Korea. Its members debate Korean politics and raise money for trips to the divided country. Chaz made the journey for the first time last summer. The cousins he lodged with laughed at his American accent and his inability to keep up with their prodigious drinking.

His parents are proud of Chaz, Seung tells Aviva, as proud as they can be of what they consider a half-breed child, American-born but with dusky skin and Korean eyes. Chaz does fine in school, stays out of trouble—a straighter arrow than Seung. He has a Korean American girlfriend who is at home now with her family in Binghamton. Besides, he is that something you are born as, a Number One Son, the child who can never do an irreparable wrong. Whereas Seung, with his strong grades and his athletic abilities, plucked by his school guidance counselor to apply to Auburn . . . Seung makes a bitter clicking sound.

The house is modest and not well heated. Mrs. Jung wears a thick cardigan (perhaps it is the one Seung purchased from Lands' End?) and flannel slippers.

"Should we ask if we can help in the kitchen?" Aviva wants to know.

"The last place she wants us is in her kitchen," says Seung.

They go out walking. The leaves are off the trees but still lie thickly on the ground in places, scarlet and brown. The air is warmish and damp. They pass quiet yards with fathers raking, kids tossing footballs or fooling around on skateboards. Front doors stand open: middle-class trust and leniency lie upon everything. Seung points out the town pool where, during the summers, he has a job as a lifeguard.

He tells Aviva about the time he pulled out a woman who fainted in the water and went down. He was fourteen, and, putting his mouth to hers before the paramedics arrived, he realized for the first time the full force of his desire for women. She was in her midthirties and not a picture in a magazine, not a girl with braces and new breasts. He dreamt of breaking into this woman's home, touching her jewelry, her hairbrush, her clothes. Aviva grows warm, picturing this erotic burglary, wonders if Seung has told her everything. There are times she feels he tells her, not untruths, exactly. But partial truths. He omits and conceals.

They pass the middle school Seung attended. It is an old-fashioned, comfortable-looking stone building with an ugly concrete addition. Seung has little to say about it. "A holding pen," is his comment. "A feedlot." Above the town and the long roads connecting the New Jersey suburbs to Newark lie miles of woods once inhabited by the Lenape Indians. There are rough shelters tucked inside, state campground facilities, a place where Boy Scout troops meet. Yes, Seung was once a Boy Scout.

Now Aviva knows why Seung carried a knapsack with him from the house: he takes from it a thick blanket, spreads it on the ground. They lie on their sides, face to face. He traces her features: the hairline, the small ears, the pointed chin. She smiles, drifting. Their mouths meet. She withdraws from time and space; they will lie here forever. He kisses her neck, unzips her sweater. They pull the ends of the blanket around themselves to stay warm.

A long time later, he says they must start back. His cousins will have arrived for Thanksgiving dinner, and they can set the table.

The transient warmth of bright midday has flown. It's cold now, 4:00 PM; the sun hangs behind a gray screen. Seung gives Aviva his knit cap and gloves. He tries to give her his coat, which is heavier than hers, but she refuses.

The Jungs' living room is lit up with floor and table lamps, busy. Now it's Schubert that's playing. The moment a record finishes Mr. Jung jumps up and puts a new one on. A young couple sits on the couch; the man, goateed, cradles a baby over his shoulder, swatting its bottom with affection.

"This is Vincent, my nephew, son of my sister Chansook," says Mr. Jung, but his accent is so thick that Aviva can't always understand what he's saying. Mr. Jung pours out sherry for himself, the young father, his elder son, and—with a pretense of disapproval—his younger one. The women, clearly, are expected not to drink. Seung winks at Aviva: he'll save her some. She doesn't care anyway. Since the night of the tequila, the tennis courts and the watching eyes, she has lost her taste for alcohol.

At dinner Seung coaxes her to try kimchi, the traditional Korean cabbage pickled in hot spices and garlic. "It's very hot," he warns. The family laughs as she cuts a small piece and puts it in her mouth. They are waiting for the inevitable explosion of alarm and disgust. Then they can laugh some more, at the mysterious things that separate some peoples from others. But she loves the cabbage, the heat. She asks

Seung to serve her more. The family cries out with amuse-
ment and delight, urges her to have a third helping, a fourth.

"You are an honorary Korean!" cries Mr. Jung. "You are
one of us!" He is a bit drunk. Seung shakes his head at her:
Don't be fooled.

Thoroughly pleased with their guest, this little white girl,
Jewish even, they insist on trying to teach her some Korean
words. *Bap* is rice; *cha* is tea. Chaz is Seung's *hyeong*, or elder brother. She can't make the right sounds. The words
have a bark, a snap, in their mouths that she can't re-create.
Chaz tells his parents to stop tormenting the poor girl.

"Aviva's getting tired," Seung agrees.

The men retreat with Mr. Jung to the TV room to drink
some more. Aviva holds the young couple's sleepy baby,
surprised at how heavy an infant can be. She imitates the
way his father held him, hoping she isn't squeezing too hard
or otherwise making the baby uncomfortable. She strokes
the thick soft tufts on his skull as he jams every finger except for his thumb into his mouth.

"Different drummer," the baby's mother says, and smiles,
and Aviva realizes that although she's been silent all evening there is intelligence and mischief in her eyes.

The cousins go home and Aviva and Seung help with the
dishes. Mr. Jung dozes in the easy chair. Number One Son listens to National Public Radio. Seung fills the sink, sprays the
dishes front and back, scrubs them with expert vigor. Aviva
dries, afraid of dropping and breaking something. Mrs. Jung
puts things away in the cabinets with old-fashioned glass

panes. She is silent now; something vaguely resentful drifts over to them from her broad turned back.

The guest room is under the eaves, with a slanted roof and one large bed. Aviva is too tired to unpack her suitcase. Seung removes her shoes, massages her feet. "Why can't we stay together?" she complains.

His look reprimands her. "Because my parents are Korean," he says.

She thinks it's stupid; they should put up some resistance. His parents are treating them like children. "Why should we lie about things?" she asks.

"Lying is what Korean sons do," he tells her.

The next day the family members scatter. Mrs. Jung has shopping to do, Mr. Jung is going to work for a couple of hours. Chaz is meeting some old friends. Now Aviva and Seung lie together in the bed under the eaves. He unbuttons her shirt, wrinkled and smelling of her after a couple of wearings, removes it, and arranges her for a back massage. He knows just how deep to press to produce the small pains that lead, unknotting as they go, to pleasure. He moves down the prominent spine that makes her look so frail to him from this angle, kneads her sides. He will not miss an inch of her. He takes off her jeans and massages her legs, too, and her arms, and then returns to her neck, which is soft now, floppy like a cloth doll's. He knows how to unlock her.

Later—they are both naked, sweaty, entwined—she asks him again to enter her. He doesn't answer at first. Then he stirs heavily, frowning. She settles onto her back, already having decided not to reach for or mention the condoms she brought in her knapsack. She doesn't want to interrupt their rhythm. Perhaps that was what caused his failure last time. He'll come in, the great thing will happen, and then she can stop him and get him to put on the protection. It will be all right. Seung prods at her. He is hard, but even in her inexperience she suspects he is not hard enough. The more he pushes at her, the more he seems to melt away from her, the less she can feel him. They move to a new position and for a moment he is revived, but in the end this does no good either. Anger stirs in her: How can he deny her again? Is she not offering herself to him? What is it about her that he refuses to accept? The sheets are moist with the long afternoon of their clinging and effort. A lone bird that Aviva has never and will never be able to name calls outside the window. She rolls away from Seung, her body still involuntarily sealed, undiscovered. He stretches out behind her, holds her around the waist, shaking with dry tears. She cannot spare any kindness for him; the shame feels too deep. It is as if he has denounced her in front of a crowd. She lies stiffly; the fine, fair day is an assault. Seung detaches himself and leaves the room. She hears running water downstairs. A long time. He comes and sits facing her, cross-legged, on the bed. He is wearing faded jeans and a loose white T-shirt. His hair is wet and slicked back.

"Hit me," he says.

"What?"

"H-hit me. Hit me right in the face."

He's crazy; she won't do such a thing.

"I d-deserve it. I'll feel better."

He scares her sometimes. She shakes her head. She thinks of getting up to leave, but where, in this house or out, can she go without him? None of the rooms are familiar, are places where she belongs and has the right to sit, to touch things. The only room that makes sense to her is this room, the only place that feels hers is this bed. Soon Mrs. Jung will return with her packages, Mr. Jung will sit with the paper and pour a drink. They will try to make conversation with her but the conversation will flag, neither side knowing how to keep it going. Aviva digs in her pack and pulls out a book her English teacher, Mr. Salter, mentioned once, praising it so enthusiastically that she had to go out and buy it at the Academy bookstore. *Swann's Way*, by Marcel Proust. She is washed over with relief at the recollection of this solution, the solution of stories. Proust pulls her along line by line, forcing her to pay the closest attention as he casts his sentences out and reels them back, making them quiver and loop and finally settle. The sentences hold and quiet her. She curls up on her side, opens the book to where she left off. *But he could never summon up courage to leave Paris, even for a day, while Odette was there. The weather was warm; it was the finest part of the spring.* In a matter of seconds she has both broken with and reattached herself to the sad world; she is free.

At 4:00 PM Seung interrupts her. Where has he been, what has he been doing? Maybe he took a walk; she does not inquire. It is getting close to dinnertime and he says they need to make a show of offering to help. Maybe they will run to the supermarket for a forgotten drink or vegetable. Aviva doesn't have a license; Seung will take the wheel. By bedtime, she will be pressing kisses on him again; she can't help herself. He'll forget his shame in the pure pleasure of exploring her mouth, of running his hands down her smooth flat belly and over the fullness of her hips, both generous and hard, startling in the way you can feel the bones inside.

The last morning, as a tribute to Aviva, Seung drives into town and picks up bagels, cream cheese, tomatoes. I saw him there, at Benny's Bagels, asking for sesame, poppy, and plain. We greeted each other, learned we would be taking the same train back to Boston. The Roach Coach, the kids called it; you could smoke and drink freely, the Amtrak conductors never interfered. Seung told me Aviva was staying with his family. He stuttered a bit when he was in a hurry or anxious or happy. He seemed to be all three right now. I lived on the opposite side of the valley running through the middle of town, the side where the bigger houses were. I pictured Aviva moving through the rooms of Seung's home, that thick hair of hers filled with the scents of the day: the household cooking, her perfume, decomposing leaves.

My own girlfriend was visiting, Lisa Flood; I told him so, to make it clear Aviva's presence in his home gave him nothing up on me. I watched him jog to his parents' double-parked car. Have I spoken about the way Seung walked? He was slightly flat-footed; his center of gravity was low and his feet splayed a bit. I wondered why no one at Auburn seemed to notice this obvious flaw, the way we had in middle school.

Nights in my own house my mother no longer shared the Judge's bedroom. The guest room had become her own; she'd re-wallpapered it in red and black roses, deep bloody tones. Lisa had my brother Dan's old bedroom, still filled with his hockey trophies, his school achievement awards. The bastard had to frame and mount every one of them; it looked like a physician's office. Nine, ten o'clock, my mother already drunk and in bed, the Judge reading biographies of famous jurists and politicians, I came into Lisa's room and lay on top of her. Before we arrived at my parents' I'd determined that on this vacation from the campus (for Lisa was one for the rules; she would never have agreed to close a door meant to be open, or sneak off to an illicit location) I would finally take her virginity. And she mine, although I had never let on to her that this would be the outcome. The previous year I had been courtly if a little grumpy, acceding to Lisa's pleas that we ought to wait, it wasn't yet the right time . . . I had been sure, like any sap, that my patience would eventually be rewarded.

But now, with my memories of the boathouse, of what it had felt like to be pressed up against Aviva, desperate to sink in, I no longer wanted to fuck Lisa so that I could enjoy what there was to enjoy and take what there was to take, or even so I could finally see myself as a man. I wanted Lisa so that I could close my eyes and pretend that she was Aviva, imagine losing myself part by part and being submerged. Maybe, in fact, I didn't want either one of them, just that sensation of self being stripped away until there was nothing left. I coaxed and coaxed Lisa until she finally gave way, on Thanksgiving evening. She was very still beneath me, attempting with smiles alternating with winces to be encouraging if not enthusiastic. So patient, such a trooper. By the third night I was lifting her legs and wrapping them around me so that she was bent almost perpendicular, so I could drive farther, disappear further. But I could not *get* further, could not obliterate either myself or her, and my frustration mounted: I began to hate her. The poor girl: a nice girl, not a terribly pretty girl, with blond brittle hair and pale skin dotted with blemishes. Her bottom already heavy and middle-aged, defeated-looking in her tan corduroys. She must have wondered what the ferocity was about. I told myself she would think it was for her, her boyfriend driven to frenzies by her appeal or by his worship, but I'm sure she was far too smart for that. She was a very smart girl. She became a doctor—an endocrinologist, as it happens—married, and had four children. Four children! I was startled as they began to arrive, at regular two-year intervals, in the pages of the *Auburn Bulletin*. I am sure she is a very good mother, and I pray she has a husband who respects and admires her, and who craves her matronly buttocks and breasts. I imagine she does. I always detected that she had the dignity and self-respect to choose someone more full-hearted than me.

Home with the car, Seung carries in the bags of food. Chaz left the previous evening, to pick up his girlfriend in Binghamton and return with her to school. The mood around the table, with its red-checked breakfast cloth, is festive. On the brink of Seung and Aviva's departure, the four of them find enough to say to each other. The Jungs like bagels as much as any good Jewish family. At the research facility where Mr. Jung works (virology: later he will be one of the first researchers to isolate the new virus called HIV), people bring in platters of them for birthdays and other celebrations. Seung slices the tomatoes—"Gentile lox," he says—and makes with them a pretty arrangement. Aviva agrees the tomatoes on top of cream cheese taste good. She and the Jungs banter about the train ride back to Boston. They want to know does she have enough money for the meal car, does she have a good book to read (they have noticed how often she has her nose in a novel; does she also read serious books like the new biography of Nikola Tesla?), what time will the shuttle bus arrive back at Auburn? And are Aviva's parents pleased with how she is doing in school? There is much to talk about; why didn't any of them notice that before? Mrs. Jung's round face looks benevolent, positively maternal. Mr. Jung gently teases the girl: His son must make sure she puts on some weight when she returns to school; she is too skinny! Does she have a portion of meat every day? "Eat kimchi!" he cries when he drops the two young people at the station, waving his arms around. "It will make you strong!"

18

We run into Voss at Penn Station, Lisa and I, on the way back to school. He and his mother live in a big penthouse in the East Eighties. His father died of a heart attack when he was a kid; he doesn't have siblings. I've seen this penthouse all of once. Although I'm supposedly one of Voss's closest friends, on vacations he is somehow always too busy with his old St. Albans classmates and their fast Spence and Brearley girlfriends to remember to invite me to the booze- and blow-soaked parties he throws. The funny thing is that Voss's mother is a serious, serious teetotaler. I know this because the one time I was over I saw AA paraphernalia all about the place—the *Big Book* in both the kitchen and the living room, the Serenity Prayer in the bathroom. Voss explained that his mom had been active in AA for years, was a sponsor to many other members, and had even become something called a general service representative, meaning she went to conferences all over the country. It's because of this regular travel that Voss has an empty apartment in which to host his bacchanalia. You have to ask yourself if it's really possible his mother doesn't know. The disarrangement of things even after obsessive cleanups, the leftover fumes . . . Maybe Mrs. V finds some perverse satisfaction in letting her son live out the dissolution she's sworn off.

Voss looks like he hasn't slept for a week. Maybe he hasn't. His old friends are dreaming hangover dreams in their comfy beds, getting ready to return to their day school lives, so he's suddenly willing to enjoy my inferior conversation and company. It's the kind of morning that makes me wonder, once again, how it is that Voss thinks himself so superior to me. In middle school I swam with one of the cooler crowds; something about my family and its longevity in our town kept me in its company, even though the girls in the group often opined that I was "so negative." I expected Auburn to be a simple continuation of that. When it comes down to it, I have a better pedigree than Voss or many of his day school friends. At a place like Auburn, you'd think that would matter, and for generations it *did* matter, but somehow, by the time I arrived, it didn't so much anymore.

The Dramat is partly to blame, I know that. Taking part in the productions now and again is fine, if it's seen as just for fun, or if you're a girl. If you're a guy, and you really *care* . . . My passion for the theater nudged me into the category of kid who is a bit suspect, whom you can snub when the mood takes you.

Lisa dislikes Voss very much. She thinks he's coarse and a bully, and who can really disagree? Cort doesn't rub her quite so much the wrong way; at least he makes an effort to include her in his jokes and to sound out her opinions. Voss, for his part, doesn't take too much trouble to hide the fact that he considers Lisa even more socially negligible than me. She's too earnest, right-minded, and intelligent— all things Voss, on some level, knows he is not. You may be wondering how it is that I myself would end up with such an earnest and right-minded girl. And what such a girl would want with me. But there is more connecting the two of us than it might seem. Lisa genuinely enjoys theater, for one thing. And I can find it a relief to be with someone apparently devoid of my primary personality trait, sourness. As for what Lisa gets out of it, all I can say is that her choices, like mine, are rather limited. Neither of us has been anointed as one of Auburn's Top Sweethearts.

Lisa is silent as we follow Voss into one of the rearmost train cars. It's an axiom that the farther back the car, the noisier it is and the more drinking that goes on. I can see that Lisa hates the raucous laughter, and she tenses as Voss keeps needling her to accept a swig of his Wild Turkey. When a kid who must have started the day with a cocktail throws up just past Stamford, she says it's time to move. Frankly I'm ready for a little quiet myself. The headache I always develop when I visit home is going into its fifth day and is outstripping Extra-Strength Tylenol's ability to keep it in check.

We have already seated ourselves four cars up when I notice Aviva and Seung a few rows ahead, and by then it's too late to invent an excuse to move again. Aviva sits against the

window, smiling as she watches Connecticut roll by. The
two hold hands: very sweet. I'm surprised to see them here,
away from the party atmosphere Seung loves, but perhaps
Aviva, like Lisa, was in charge of seating arrangements today. After a while, Mac MacMillan, a kid who apparently
likes a solitary and meditative toke, passes Seung a joint; he
takes a brief hit and then holds it out to Aviva, who shakes
her head. He bends and puffs a little smoke into her ear.
She squirms and smacks him playfully. Their eyes meet.
He leans to kiss her. They don't gobble and pant like other
couples you see on the train, and their discretion stabs me
more than flaunting would. They give off something of
the vibe of the long-together couple who are Getting It so
often that they don't need to show off. They part every so
often to gaze at each other, Aviva lifting her hand to stroke
Seung's cheek. She smiles; he doesn't. He's in too deep to
smile. "You like watching, huh?" says someone across from
me, some prep or lower punk I don't even recognize. I fix
him with a stare; he snorts and looks away. Lisa, reading her
biology textbook, pretends not to hear.

19

Seung has got his hands on something new. Quaaludes, he tells her; methaqualone if you want to know the scientific name. There are four medium-sized white pills taped inside a packet of white tissue paper. Seung goes to the library—the public library, not the Academy library—to research the stuff he and his friends put into their bodies. It's not so much that he's concerned about his health, just that he likes to see the molecular diagrams with their long, hyphenated names, to memorize the chemical formulas and know that chlorine destroys LSD molecules on contact. It's not useful information, but it interests him, perhaps as much as does the experience of alteration. In these explorations you can see in him the son his father wished to raise, the one who understands that science is the only truly reputable calling for a son. Seung is pulling Bs in chemistry only because he has an aptitude for memorization. He takes it on his father's insistence. The urgency of it all escapes him. But the poetry of ingested substances engages him: *Bioavailability. Metabolism. Half-life.*

"What will it do to me?" asks Aviva.

If it's good stuff, he explains, you go into a kind of trance, in which all the world seems benevolent and amusing. You love everyone.

And if it's not good stuff?

You just get relaxed, he assures her.

It's a Saturday in early December. They're in his room. He wanted to go to the Bog, but she refused; it's way too cold and she doesn't like being around other kids who are half out of their minds with whatever they're on. He swallows his pills first, to give her confidence. She doesn't ask where he got the drugs. Seung, Sterne, Giddings, Detweiler: the pack of them returned from Thanksgiving break with supplies replenished. They have contacts at home. At Auburn, it's harder: tricky to trust the townies, with whom there's always the factor of resentment; Academy students have been double-crossed. And Auburn the town is very small, a hard place to keep secrets. The last thing anyone needs is a couple of police officers showing up at the dean of students's office, asking questions. So, better to stock up over vacations.

Why should a kid like Seung, a proctor in his dorm, able student, musician, swimmer, bound for a lesser Ivy or a good small liberal arts college, why should he risk himself, why should he spend so much time in the pursuit and exploration of illicit substances? What is he looking for? Or avoiding? Is he motivated by an unhealthy need for excitement? Feelings of inadequacy? An impulse toward self-destruction? No, no, the older generation has the wrong vocabulary altogether; they are blinded by concepts like *illegality* and *addiction* and maybe even *sin*. Seung's passion for intoxication has to do with his discovery, that very first time an older kid passed a spliff to him at a middle school football game, that there is something behind or beyond what ordinary experience presents to him, something he privately calls *the inside*. Only rarely does that inside reveal itself; mostly it teases him with transient glimmers of radiant energy in a field of grass, the panting of a dog, the mute mouth of a doorway. But when it comes in full he has the sensation of touching reality, or at least a reality more real than the one available to him day by day. There is an end to the unease, the sense he has of never being at home. During these times of illumination he sees himself as comical, but it's a sympathetic view, not a disdainful one. He has no family, no constricting allegiances; he is simply one golden child of the universe. He can see the suffering of each fellow creature like a brilliant steam rising from the pores, a nimbus terrible and exquisite at once. It's the suffering that makes each person beautiful, like a bracelet, like a cage. He has enormous compassion for everyone, and the fact that the suffering will continue, that he can do nothing about it, does not unduly distress him. This is simply how things must be.

It is at these times that Seung sees, in the hollow of his palm or hiding in a stand of trees, the things that later he must make—the drawings of leopards with golden eyes, the perfect spheres carved out of wood.

Seung's words tempt Aviva. She too would like to go somewhere else, to see into the nature of things. She would like her
heart to open; she would like to see the astonishing colors
Seung speaks of. She would like beauty to supplant fear.

But she *is* afraid. She suspects that in the honeycomb of
her subconscious brain there do not, in fact, lie caverns of
benevolence and fellow feeling. Rather, she expects there
are evil things lurking there: rage, a lust for conquest, cru-
elty. Why would she want to loosen the chains? Here is a
girl for whom even the phantasms of movies are too much,
sometimes, to endure. She's learned to say no to thrillers,
gangster films, anything having to do with supernatural
powers or aliens. Anything along those lines terrorizes her,
makes her clutch her head as if the control and good sense
in it might be sucked away.

Seung lends her books to read, trying to explain where
he's coming from: Aldous Huxley's *The Doors of Perception*,
Albert Hofmann on LSD.

"Nothing can happen," Seung promises. "I'll be with you
the whole time." But that's not good enough, she thinks. He
can't be *inside her mind*, where the caverns are. She could
wander away from him down there, out of his protective
grasp. She—her very being—might be stolen.

She says she's sorry, really, really sorry, but no. No
Quaaludes. No nothing.

He badgers her for a while, is gloomy and disappointed,
then lets it go.

20

When I began to piece together this account, I did so simply to make sense of things, to create a plausible whole out of the fragments left behind after Seung's death. Later, as I amplified and embroidered (yet every little detail, every flourish I added seemed to bring me closer to the truth), I began to see my tale as a kind of restitution, the only type of penance I could then see to pay Aviva. An attempt to understand her—or rather, to allow her complexity to grow beyond the possibility of my understanding. And to Seung also I owed—well, everything. As long as Aviva was only what I thought she was (Seung's sex kitten, tease, the girl stolen from me by those who thought themselves my betters), and as long as Seung was only what I thought *he* was (the thief, the golden boy who'd plumbed the depths of a woman and got to go back for more and more), then I could still say to myself, *They got what they deserved.* I needed to see *who they were*, to strip the myth from them, and that is what I labored to do, year by year, piece by piece.

There's another aspect of this, too. Only very far along in this labor of construction did I glean that there was an affinity between Aviva and me that went beyond whatever I had been trying to get out of her and she out of me. I saw that there was something in her dilemma of my own. I've never wholly believed in love, and perhaps that's why, over the years, women have gone in and out of my life, sometimes quickly, sometimes staying for long enough that there is talk (fortunately eventually cut short) of marriage, a future. Before they leave, these women take the time, a great deal of time, to tell me exactly what is wrong with me, above all what they perceive as my failure to feel. How can I explain that it is not precisely that? I could tell them about a time when I felt altogether too much—too much desire, too much rage. If I did, would I receive some sort of compassionate exemption? To be perfectly frank, I've never thought that any of these women have themselves been good and kind and feeling enough to be entrusted with my story. I hope to meet the right listener one day, the one I can unburden myself to. Perhaps then things will change, or I will be forgiven for being unable to change.

Why do women say the things about men that they do? It's not only my disappointed partners. Many of my female colleagues, when the conversation turns to love, are inclined to say, *Oh, all men are like that*—by which they mean defended in a certain way, inexpressive. But I know they are wrong. I know that certain men, like Seung, do not defend themselves when it would be better if they could. And certain women, like Aviva, can't find in themselves the thoroughgoing surrender that they think would make them happy and whole. Perhaps the years since have reassured Aviva, given her that soul-shaking union, or maybe she's learned that there are other ways of feeling, more natural to her, that deserve to be ennobled by the word *love*. But I wonder if it could really be so. All this time Aviva has surely believed that Seung died because of her. What has that done to her?

21

An envelope arrives from Aviva's brother, stuffed with his drawings. There are figures on skateboards: boys, but with the heads of wolves—fanged, scowling—and wings. The boys wear the same kind of T-shirts Marshall wears: dark, with the baroque insignias of Jethro Tull or the Grateful Dead. In the postures of the figures Marshall has successfully captured his dream of great speed. They are flying, somersaulting, their long hair streaming behind them. Accompanying the drawings is a short letter. Marshall tells Aviva that he is growing his hair long. *Mom hasn't said anything.* Then he mentions that he was beaten up by three older kids from school, ninth graders. It happened in the park; he'd decided to take a walk before getting on the bus home. He'd been lost in thought, didn't see them coming. He'd been thinking about a skateboard move called a Bert Revert, rehearsing it in his head. His arm was broken but he's otherwise fine. The principal wanted to know who the kids were, but he hasn't told. Anyway, it's all worked out okay; he and the three boys have made up, nothing more will happen. With Marshall it is always as if Aviva's reading a foreign language, in which the words don't signify the customary things. This is not because Marshall is cagey or deceptive. He means precisely what he says. Moreover, one learns to believe him. Somehow, this twelve-year-old boy has had—if she knows Marshall—an unexceptional, even pleasant talk with his three attackers and everything has been amicably settled. Nothing more *will* happen, and none of the adults will ever know what did happen in the first place.

Aviva takes the letter with her to the dining hall. She eats lunch on the late side so that she can wait for Seung while he finishes kitchen duty. He has a work-study job three days a week. He rinses dishes, loads the two huge dishwashers, wipes down counters, mops the floor. When Mr. Carlton, the dining hall supervisor, isn't there, Aviva follows the conveyor belt into the kitchen and visits. She likes to watch Seung's muscular arms plunged deep into the sudsy yellow water. The femininity of the task throws his masculinity into relief. It is the same with his skin—satin, hairless—which only sculpts his swollen biceps and thick wrists more nakedly. His arms, so capable, so bent to his duty, stir her profoundly. She slips behind him and wraps her own around his waist. It pleases her to think that the other kitchen lackeys may grumble at this exhibitionism. Let them; she is happy. She lays her cheek on Seung's back. If Mr. Carlton is present she instead sits in the empty dining hall drinking cup after cup of weak coffee. She does not eat enough at her meal: perhaps a slice of American cheese, a slice of bologna, a smear of mustard. She can't say why. The coffee is what fills her, but after a while it gives her the shakes. She is light, disoriented.

When Seung is done she accompanies him to the pool. They walk out of the dark, cloudy afternoon into the well-lit mouth of the gymnasium. The hall is wide and high and even on overcast days sun seems to stream in from the skylights. One can hear hollow thwacks from the hockey rink, the muffled slap of water against poolside, footfalls and shouts from the basketball courts. Who gave the money for all of this amplitude? It costs so much more, unthinkably more, to make a building not just serviceable but solid and beautiful. Someone has thought it worthwhile. In return his name is carved above the entrance: Arthur J. Eggleton IV.

Next door is the old gym, a dimly lit building with nets hanging from the ceiling to hold footballs and basketballs, a balcony converted into a running track. You can practically see the boys of bygone days with their leather football helmets and their skin scrubbed with harsh soap, lines of boys facing off, staring each other down, grappling and wrestling: a damper, danker time, a time without girls or women. The competition between boys must have been something purer then, less veiled and more prized.

Aviva sits in the stands reading Julio Cortázar, *Hopscotch*, in which the chapters may be read in any order. The impishness of this delights her. When she reads she unconsciously tears off the corners of the pages and chews on them like bits of gum. Her books all look like mice have gotten at them. Seung's teammates gaze up at this girl, so carnal, so oblivious, so unimpressed. They wonder how in the hell a girl like that ever ended up with a slanty-eyed kid like Seung.

How the kids used to hassle Seung in our middle school. "Butt-sniffing," we called it: figuring out who the alphas were going to be. I hadn't known Seung before. There weren't that many Asians in our town, and most were the classic type: scrawny, bespectacled, very down with their math and science homework. If you had a name like Jim or John, you had a chance, but Li-Yu or Seung . . . I remember Seung getting grabbed in the hallways, called a sneaky Chink. Someone would turn out his pockets, remove his lunch money and breath mints. Teachers weren't like they are today, didn't care what went on in the hallways, who got beaten up. I probably would have been beaten up more often myself if it weren't for my family. It's not as if the other sixth graders really knew or cared that the Bennett-Joneses were landed gentry as far back as the 1700s, that one of my great-great-grandfathers had been on the Supreme Court and another had been lieutenant governor of Rhode Island. And yet kids somehow absorb, who knows how, a sense of caste. So although I was pudgy and had kooky blond curls, although I wasn't particularly good at any sports besides Frisbee, if that even counted as a sport, I was left more or less alone. I had my crowd and I kept my more suspect inclinations, like Dungeons & Dragons and New Wave music, under wraps. I was well above a Seung in the pecking order. When we got to Auburn, the two of us, I couldn't understand how he rose so high, so free of his name and his looks, how he became a leader, while I was just some other guy from the joke state of New Jersey.

Seung enters the pool area in his team's crimson Speedo. His primary event is the butterfly. It's a stroke that makes no sense to Aviva: the swimmer seems to be sending himself backward nearly as much as forward. The whistle blows and Aviva watches six boys plunge simultaneously under the water. The swimmers rise slick and gasping, slam down again after capturing the air. Up once more. Seung's arms move like the wheels on a crooked axle. It's a quick race, only one length, no time for her to look away. She tracks his black head now leading, now lagging. The whistle shrills again; Seung hits the wall second. The first boy leaps out of the water. There is no trace in him of fatigue. Water sloshes off him in sheets. He is lean-legged for a swimmer, with small buttocks in his brown-and-white-striped suit. One by one the other swimmers heave themselves from the water. Seung will be pleased with his second-place finish. He neither expects nor aims to win, which is not the same as saying he does not push himself to his limits. It is just that he is no star. His value is in his dependability. His performance is steadily strong without being outstanding. He doesn't complain about 6:00 AM practices or about swimming until his arms burn and seize. When the coach says grunt, he grunts. He never loses his temper. I am a team player, he tells her. That's what I am.

22

My mother and the Judge drive up to see the Sunday afternoon performance of my *Macbeth*. I've cast the show against type, with big Janny Pettigrew, with her long teeth and rounded shoulders, as Lady Macbeth. For weeks I had to work training the whinny out of her. She laughed at inapt moments. Lady Macbeth doesn't laugh, I told her. Yreni Arsov, who was used to being the diva in Auburn productions, who'd been Masha in *Three Sisters*, I gave the part of Lady Macduff. Lady MacD has, I believe, nineteen lines. I watched Yreni struggle to lace in all that vanity and frustration as she acted the sensible, affectionate wife and mother, and I congratulated myself, I thought the result good. For Macbeth I did the best I could: Peter Malkin, short and round and blond-curled like me, an unprepossessing warrior and king. But Peter drew it out of himself. I saw that he was the one, of the whole cast, who would go on, that in

years to come we'd be reading about him. When he entered
with the bloody daggers and said, "I have done the deed.
Didst thou not hear a noise?" I saw what he had brought
up in himself, a true mean troubled desire to kill. He frightened himself, the poor boy. It made the play. People shifted
in their seats, uncomfortable. The curtain fell; at first no
one would cheer for Peter. They clapped slowly, solemnly.
The unhealth, the evil, clung to his person. Then the audi-
ence began to shake off its daze, recognize the actor in the
part. The applause grew louder and louder; people whistled
and stamped; they almost screamed. In the green room Peter laid his sword on the props table, ran his sweaty hands
through his dusty hair. For a while no one went near and he
remained entirely alone. He'd marked himself; he'd entered
the art of the thing and none of us would ever be able to see
him as innocent again.

I watch for Aviva in the audiences of our three performances; I do not see her. Cort comes the second night,
dragging Voss; they give their quick congratulations and
disappear, turning down my invitation to stay for the cast
party. My actors praise me at the party, lifting their Tabs
and Sprites, and I believe they are sincere; not all of them
like me, but they can see that I drove them, in inventive and
devious ways, to their best performances. I enjoy their ad-
miration without feeling fed by it, for the part of them that I
understand and can speak to was shed with their costumes
and face paint, and as Lisa and I circulate amid our excited,
chatting classmates, I feel as out of place as she likely does.

On Sunday, after the last show, the Judge takes my
mother and Lisa and me to the Auburn Inn, orders us clam
chowder and roast beef. He does not ask me how my college applications are going. It is understood that I will be
going to Dartmouth, his alma mater. My grades are just
good enough, and I test well. The Judge gives thousands of
dollars each year to the alumni fund. On the sly I am sending applications to Bard, Oberlin, and NYU, places with
theater programs I'm interested in. There's another thing
I haven't told him yet—I'm not going out for crew again in
the spring. I'll be spending that extra time at the Dramat.
Even Lisa doesn't know.

"That boy . . ." says the Judge.

"Who?"

"The Macbeth boy. He was a little short for the role,
didn't you think? A little pudgy."

"Yes," I say.

"The girl who played Lady Macbeth wasn't too bad."

"I thought she was very good," says Lisa. She fishes for
my hand under the table.

My mother finishes her Rob Roy before the appetizers
arrive. She signals to the waiter for another one.

"I'll have a glass of cabernet," I add, before the waiter can
go.

"You will not," says the Judge.

The waiter looks from one of us to the other. An old
man, patient, a little bent in the knees. He has seen all this
before. My mother sips neatly from her water glass.

"He's not eighteen until February the third," my father informs the waiter.

"Oh, go ahead and let him, Malcolm," says my mother.

"That's all right," I tell her.

"Where are you applying to college?" my mother asks Lisa, after she has some of the second drink inside her. She is in that phase of the evening where she is still happy, listening to some tinkly music in her head. She smiles impersonally.

"Um, Yale, Harvard, Brown . . ."

"Ah, then, you and Bruce will be apart next year."

"Well, there are the vacations," says Lisa. She squeezes my hand again. Her palms are always clammy. "And I'm a good letter writer."

"I'm sure you are," says the Judge. I can see that he'd like the food to come so that there's something in my mother to ground the booze. As if I'm a puppet and he's pulled a string, I casually slide the bread basket in my mother's direction.

The room is filling up. Our reservation was on the early side, the way the Judge likes it. I see my math teacher, Mr. Willis, sitting opposite his wife. They lift and lower their utensils in a companionable silence. I smell lobster bisque at other tables. I would have liked some lobster bisque. They make it with sherry here.

"We're going to Boston in the morning," the Judge tells Lisa. Now that she's been dispatched to a different part of the country for her college years, he feels friendlier to her.

"Oh, what will you be doing?" she asks politely.

"The Fine Arts Museum, of course, and then we have special passes to the new John F. Kennedy Library, which we have not yet seen."

"The museums in Boston really are inferior," comments my mother.

We talk of museums and cities and I have the feeling that none of us, even my father, actually knows what he is talking about, is sure of the truth of even his least statement. When we cannot think of things to say about museums and cities, we talk about the food. My mother orders two more drinks.

The waiter clears away our dishes and hands a dessert card to each of us.

"Cherry cream pie!" cries my mother. "It has been so long since I've had cherry cream pie!"

I'm worried; I can see the haze coming up in her eyes. Some memory, some fragment of childhood has been suddenly retrieved; I don't want to hear what it is.

The Judge's hand comes down on her small, fragile one like a clamp. "Very good then, we'll order you the pie."

Lisa orders a lemon sherbet—she watches her weight. I should watch mine, too, but I get a brownie à la mode, out of general ill temper. The Judge orders a Drambuie, his standard after-dinner drink. "I'll share it with you, lovie," he says to my mother. Her smile trembles. I know what he's doing—claiming the drink for both of them so that she can't order another of her own. I can see the rest of their evening. She'll draw a scalding bath and lie in it, her skin reddening, the hot fumes inducing a confusion and sleepiness reassuringly akin to that of inebriation. The Judge will call out from the bedroom, where he is reading the *New York Times*. He will quote President Carter and Brzezinski, and say just what he thinks of what they've said. He will ask her what she thinks of what he thinks of what they've said, but she won't answer. Every ten minutes or so he will heave himself out of his chair and knock lightly on the bathroom door, on the pretext of seeing if she needs some soap or an extra towel, but really in order to make sure that she has not drowned. And perhaps on one of those visits he will steal a glimpse of the hair between her legs, the naked soft thighs. She is still shapely, still youthful when all is said and done, just a shade past fifty. On those evenings when she looks at him with clear eyes, remembering who he is, who she is, he is glad to come back to her.

23

The students exit the day's last class into darkness. Six thirty, and the dining hall is a brilliant bubble of glass. Aviva sits with her friends, Seung with his. Afterward they walk in the snow. Aviva's toes and fingers always hurt in the cold. She wears boots with fur linings, the thickest she can find.

Seung shows her yet another of the secret places he knows. The Science Building is built into a hill, leaving a crawl space beneath one corner of the foundation. A steam pipe exits into the crawl space; the temperature in there must be eighty degrees. They wedge themselves under the slanting foundation, unzip their jackets. The gravel floor is not uncomfortable. They can sit here, unseen, watching the snow fall, stripped down to their shirts. Outside, the lit snow, the dark figures exiting the buildings.

"It's beautiful," Aviva says.

She unbuttons his shirt, warming her hands on his chest. He leans his head against the dirty concrete wall. She never fails to be stirred by this gesture of his, the way he bares his throat to her, like a dog acknowledging the stronger creature in a fight. It strikes her to her depths. She kisses him gently, then imperiously, crawling onto his lap and holding him fiercely around the waist with her legs.

The paths have emptied. The snow is thickly cratered with footprints that cross this way and that and fall into each other. Aviva and Seung emerge into a private field. He stands behind her in the tracks, his wide hands on her shoulders. He takes three large steps away from her.

"Stand tall," he says. "Keep your arms straight at your sides. Like a board."

He knows she'll do it on the first try. Her trust in him is absolute. Obediently she lets herself fall. She watches the dark sky rise up over her and then rush away again. Then she lies, safe, in Seung's hands.

"Again," she murmurs.

They do it over and over. But they agree she can't catch him; he weighs so much more than she does.

24

A week before the Christmas break Aviva buys an enamel mug for each girl in Hiram and fills it with M&M's, Hershey's Kisses, miniature Reese's cups, caramels, peppermints, licorice sticks. The slashed bags of sweets carpet her room. She bought too much and doesn't know what to do with it all. She spent a long time in the drugstore, comparing the heavy packages glittering with colored foil. She was first drawn to the aisle by a pressing desire to treat herself, to bring a bag of M&M's back to her room and gorge on it until her head swam and her hands shook with sugar tremors. At the same time she told herself no, no, you mustn't, and so she stood there, paralyzed, unable to make the purchase, unable to leave the store.

Then the brilliant solution occurred to her. There was a way to have all of these delights and not sicken herself, not just the M&M's but the Kisses and caramels and everything else, a way to handle the lovely wrappings and inundate her room with the smell of chocolate, mint, and raspberry. The candy would not be for her but for others. How wonderful! But when she carried her armloads to the counter, her confidence faltered; she believed the cashier lady could see right through her to the insatiable greed inside. The amount on the register was so high that Aviva had to go back to the bank for more money.

For two nights she stays up very late, drawing the name of each girl onto a mug with thick metallic ink. Her roommate is sleeping and the overhead light is off; her desk lamp shines a small bright circle on her careful industry. She feels like the girl Rumpelstiltskin trapped in a room to spin hay into gold. She is dazzled by the riches all around her. Every so often, when she cannot bear it anymore, she unwraps a Kiss and places it in her mouth, closes her eyes, and stops her elfin work for a while. The result is such a flood of want that she has to lie down and grip the metal foot of her cot until the impulse to tear at the packages with her teeth and stuff unwrapped candies into her mouth, swallowing paper and foil, passes. She manages to hang on, shuddering.

The night before holiday dismissal she will leave a mug in front of each door. The thought of each girl emerging the next morning in her nightgown, with her toothbrush and face cream in hand, to find her gift, fills her with unspeakable pleasure and justifies all the pain of the preparations. To make sure she will not touch the leftovers—every mug has been stuffed to the brim—she gathers the extra sweets and dumps them into a shoe box which she leaves by the sick elm tree behind Hiram for the squirrels. Within hours there are bright scraps all over the yard, the birds diving and screaming and pecking at each other, and even the box itself has been gnawed at and scattered. Señora Ivarra, Hiram's dorm head, is furious, convenes a dormitory meeting. Aviva raises her hand and turns herself in. A would-be fornicator, an accomplice to drug use, a sneak, and this is what she is finally publicly reprimanded for: littering. She weeps, genuinely ashamed. The other girls stare at her, aghast. "Whatever gave you the idea?" asks the señora. Aviva shakes her head, cannot look the señora in the eye, lest the señora see the flecks of frenzy there.

25

For Christmas break I rent a car and drive myself home to Jordan. I need to avoid the train, the possibility of seeing Seung and Aviva there again. I don't know that they are already on their way to Chicago. When I hit the New Jersey state line I find I can't bear to face everyone just yet: the Judge, my mother, my brother Dan—Andy and his wife are with her family in Maine. I am supposed to be home in time for dinner. I drive beyond my exit, my mood lightening as I cross into Warren County and then Pennsylvania. When I reach the Poconos I have to ask myself where am I planning to go, what is the point? It is past eight o'clock. I turn around.

My father answers the doorbell. "You might have stopped at a pay phone," he says. My mother comes up behind him, her face pale and depleted now that the day's makeup is scrubbed away. To my surprise I find myself apologizing repeatedly, a wetness coming up in my eyes. "Now, now," my mother trills, happy to have something to do or say. "It's all right. You'd think you'd committed a crime."

26

The streets of New York are lined with a gray, shimmering slush, a slush the color of a rich lawyer's tie. There are hours before the flight that will take them to Chicago. They are departing from here rather than Boston because Aviva's mother found a good deal on tickets out of LaGuardia. Aviva doesn't remember her mother ever using the phrase "a good deal" before. She and Seung walk along Madison and Lexington Avenues, but stop in few stores: the slim saleswomen and fey salesmen in these tiny bright boxes do not like Aviva's purple-feathered vintage hat or Seung's canvas knapsack. When they get to Bloomingdale's they look hopelessly for a bench where Seung can massage Aviva's bloodless, stinging toes.

"This is no good," she says. "We have to find someplace else."

She knows the name of a hotel, the Dorchester; her parents used to stay there on trips to the city, the ones from which they brought back pungent cellophane bags filled with New York bagels studded with garlic and poppy seeds. It takes them a while to find a store that will let them use its White Pages. The hotel is in the East Nineties between Madison and Park. They walk there, forgoing a cab, saving their cash for food and the bus to the airport.

The lobby is large, tan, a little shabby. It surprises Aviva that her parents would have stayed here, a place not just so. Perhaps it was in better shape years ago.

Seung removes Aviva's wet boots and puts her foot in his lap. She is aware of the puddles they are making on the whorled carpet. She is wearing hand-knitted socks she bought herself as a holiday present. They were in a window on Nut Street. You hardly ever saw anything pretty in those utilitarian windows filled with envelopes, bandage boxes, crew-necked sweaters, lacrosse sticks. Auburn has yet to shed its mill town dourness, its willful lack of style.

The desk clerk, a gaunt man with a mustache and not much to do, watches Seung's hands cup Aviva's toes, press into the pad beneath the joints. Seung knuckles the arch, chafes the heel. The indifferent, skeptical gaze of the city has worn Aviva down; she feels tiny, like a child calling out to be heard at a parade. She is aware of the eyes of the man at the desk and looks up. He smiles encouragingly, malevolently.

"Let's go upstairs," she tells Seung.

They wait until the clerk wanders into the back and then take the stairs to the third floor, where they call for the elevator. They study the floor buttons: one through nineteen. "You choose," Aviva says. She is happy again.

He selects seventeen, his age. They walk along the dim corridor and into another stairwell, put down their bags.

"Now," says Seung.

They kiss, talk, kiss again. Kissing is not the right word for it, this thing that they do. *Kiss*—a term for a beach movie or a teen magazine. I looked it up in the dictionary. *To touch with the lips esp. as a mark of affection or greeting; to come in gentle contact.* As a noun: *a caress with the lips.* What Seung and Aviva are up to is more outlandish and more significant than that. You have to try to remember back to a time when fucking hadn't happened to you yet, not quite, when you still didn't even know precisely what it was (though you might have thought you did) and what it would heal in you or wouldn't. When a tongue pushing deep inside you *was* as fucked as you could possibly be. I think maybe it was, in fact, more than anything that came later . . .

And the talking has to be given its proper measure also. It is just as important, in a different way. Without it they would turn on each other, not be able to stand the pleasure. Kiss and talk . . . they never run out of things to say, Aviva and Seung. What do they talk about? What did any of us talk about in those days? Everything seemed to be of pressing interest. Friends who were in trouble and friends who were not. Studies, teachers, food eaten and anticipated, a shirt or a pair of pants worn, lost, disliked, discarded by a parent, mourned. The movies. Students one had known in past years who took on the features of heroes, remnants of the famous age just past for which we were a bit belated: the sixties, the age of true hippies and pure drugs and rebellion with glory. Tom Petty, Peter Gabriel, Neil Young, The Band, Leonard Cohen, Joan Armatrading, Traffic, Eric Clapton, Elvis Costello. This or that prep or lower whom one looked after like a brother or sister. Parents and siblings, not so much—except that Aviva often spoke of Marshall.

They are sitting on the concrete floor, knees touching, sleepy, talking, when the two men from security open the stairwell door. The boy and girl are asked what they are doing here. Aviva says that they are just talking. They have a plane to catch in three hours and nowhere to go; they are just making the time go by. The security guards do not seem satisfied with these truths. They ask the two teenagers to please come with them to the manager's office. The manager's office is large and bright; the manager himself is small. He asks what they were doing in the stairwell. Aviva repeats her explanations. The scene feels like the one that took place in Dean Ruwart's office not long ago, when he asked if she knew why she had been called in. Once again she does not know, not really.

"This hotel is private property," the manager tells them. His name is Mr. Ianetti. The statement is meaningless to Aviva. They were using a deserted stairwell, they were talking. Even if they had had their clothes half off she cannot see what they have to apologize for.

The room is neatly furnished with a polished dark-wood desk, framed botany prints, and two armchairs upholstered in striped ticking. It looks much nicer than the lobby or the corridors do. Seung and Aviva sit in the armchairs while Mr. Ianetti stands behind his desk and the men from security stand along the walls. Weak sunlight falls inside the room through cream-colored curtains. After an hour or so, when the two teenagers have answered the same questions over and over, have allowed their bags to be searched, have shown Aviva's bankbook and her father's credit card and Seung's driver's license, have offered to get Aviva's mother or father on the phone, it occurs to Aviva that these three men may detain them long enough to make them miss their plane. She shows the men their tickets again, explains their need to depart. Seung says very little. He understands that the part of an Asian boy is to be silent. Nothing he can say will instill trust. And Aviva begins to understand that the door of the room will not open until these men wish it to open. For the first time she grows uneasy. If she were older and less convinced that the world works along rational and reasonable principles, she might think to make more of the fact that her uncle is a lawyer at a large firm in Chicago. She might hint at her surprise that Mr. Ianetti would be suspicious of two students who attend the prestigious Auburn Academy. She might mention some of her family's expensive vacations: Switzerland, the Galapagos, Mexico.

But perhaps Mr. Ianetti knew from the first few minutes that there is no reason to detain them and has simply been waiting to see this uneasiness in her eyes, this fear. For suddenly he stands up and asks the two of them to promise that they will never set foot in this hotel again. If they do, he will have them arrested immediately. They promise. They scramble for their bags, and one of the security men, like a footman, opens the door for them to depart.

Out on the street Seung says, "Christ, it could have been worse—much, much worse."

"What do you mean?"

He has a quarter bag of pot tucked into the inside zip pocket of his knapsack. They didn't even look there.

She wants to strike him—the stupidity of it! What the fuck—she says that to him—was he thinking, planning to bring this shit on the plane? She pictures the knapsack passing under the X-ray camera, the operator stopping it, reversing the belt. Someone saying *I'm sorry* and asking for their boarding passes. Moreover—and she says this, too, *moreover*—was it his expectation that she was going to use this stuff with him in Chicago? What made him so sure she would say yes? Or had he been planning to go off and get high all by himself? Seung stares into the traffic. His eyes can go so hard at times. She tells him that she doesn't care how much the stuff cost, how much trouble it was to get; when they get to the airport he has to flush it down the toilet. She waves wildly for a cab—it's the only way they're going to make their flight.

He's such a child sometimes, but all the same, she admires him. He sat as naturally and easily the whole time as if there were no danger at all. If she had his fearlessness! His face betrayed nothing; he never once glanced at his bag.

27

Without speaking of it they have agreed not to try to make love again for now; they won't risk further disappointment and recriminations. They are lighthearted and happy. They sleep pressed together in Aviva's childhood bed, a four-poster with a twin mattress. The four-poster was the one girlish fantasy in which she was ever indulged. It is hung with double curtains: the inside curtain a stiff, old-fashioned white cotton with lace eyelet, the outside curtain a sheer panel that flutters in the summer when there's air conditioning. The canopy has scalloped white borders. The mattress lay so high up for the six-year-old girl that to get into bed she had to make a running leap from the other side of the room. Anya Rossner still doesn't know what got into her, that she arranged to purchase it, had the curtains made up. In the rest of the house she brooks no ornamentation, no soft, sentimental aesthetics. "You so wanted it," she says to Aviva, as if apologizing to herself.

Aviva and Seung lie in bed late and read the Sunday *New York Times*, what sections of it they can get their hands on. Mrs. Rossner always makes off with Arts, and Marshall gets Sports, which no one else wants. He also reads the news, but says he doesn't understand any of it. He comes into Aviva's room to give over the front section, and greets the lovers. Already he likes Seung, and Seung likes him. He pushes himself up onto the bed, swings his feet over the side.

The front page says that the Soviets are continuing to build up land forces at the Afghan border, apparently in preparation for an invasion. A sixty-four-foot Christmas card was delivered to the U.S. Embassy in Teheran for the fifty-three hostages.

"What's up, buddy?" asks Seung.

"Nothing. Mom says we have to leave at three thirty."

"Fine."

Silence. Seung's hand strays up the back of Aviva's neck. It grabs a hunk of hair, pulls suggestively. Aviva wriggles to move her thigh against Seung's thigh. A low growl of appreciation escapes him.

"Am I not wanted?" Marshall asks seriously.

Seung grins. "You'll be more wanted later."

When Aviva saw Marshall at the airport she couldn't help crying out. He'd shaved his head. He'd done it himself, apparently, and there were nicks and scabs especially in the back. He'd left little tufty patches, too.

"I thought you were growing your hair out," Aviva said.

He thought a moment. "I was beginning to look skanky."

They drive to the university. Mrs. Rossner drives like an

old woman, creeping up on the traffic lights, then slamming the brake pedal as if she's just narrowly averted a collision. Marshall stares moodily out the window. Aviva's never seen him like this. She wonders if her absence has left him in too difficult a position after all. He's alone in the big apartment with his mother, with no one to help him grow up.

The stone buildings at the college squat in the snow: pale, dirty, quiet. Mrs. Rossner's lecture today is on images of women in the advertisements of the 1940s. She wears a short belted jacket and severe black slacks. Her hair is coiffed weekly at the beauty parlor, swept thickly into snug waves around her face. When she stands there, so erect, so sure, with her precise, authoritative accent, the accent she acquired as a child refugee in England, you can't understand how any husband could leave her. What she might lack in softness, in subservience, she makes up in the glamor of command. She's a woman you can't take your eyes off.

"The avatar of the forties woman in visual advertising is an almost equal amalgam of masculine and feminine traits. The hair and noticeable curve at the breasts signal femininity, as do the long shapely legs—we see this in the Betty Grable craze—yet the midbody is encased in severe and boxy lines, male-imitating suits, hiding away and denying the authentic and frightening female core—the vagina, cunt, womb . . ."

"Oh, boy," says Aviva.

"She actually said *cunt*," hisses Marshall. He's blushing.

"It's worse than usual," Aviva tells Seung. "I think she's showing off for you."

Students flock the stage after the lecture. They all want a word with Anya Rossner, want her to notice them. She is among the most popular professors on campus. The accent doesn't hurt. The students' questions are anxious and horribly sincere. The answers matter, will help them negotiate this treacherous business of male, female, money, love, success, failure.

"I used to be so proud of her when I was little, sitting up in these seats," says Aviva. "I had no idea she was using all those dirty words."

"You're still proud of her," objects Marshall.

"I know it," Aviva admits. "I mean, everything she says is absolutely true."

They go out to Mrs. Rossner's favorite diner afterward, order roast beef and rice pudding. Mrs. Rossner leaves half of her roast beef on her plate, plays with her rice pudding. Occasionally she looks up at Seung as if he's someone she can't quite place, someone who just wandered in. He thinks her lecture was marvelous. His mother would have had conniptions if she'd been here. His father would have laughed till he fell off his seat. Marshall stacks the packets of sugar and Sweet'N Low. It's dark now; none of them wants to go home. None of them wants to cross the cold parking lot, get into the cold car, and drive the long lakeside roads until they arrive back at—what?

"We should go see a movie tomorrow," says Mrs. Rossner. "There's a Satyajit Ray movie at the Film Forum."

"I guess," says Aviva.

"Let's do it," says Seung enthusiastically.

"If it has subtitles I don't want to go," says Marshall.

By the time they pull into the garage beneath the apartment it is nearly nine; the garage man has gone off duty. Mrs. Rossner leaves the car in the center aisle with the key in it; John will park it for her in the morning. Aviva and Seung go upstairs. They'll stay up until one, two o'clock, caressing, talking, falling silent, talking again. Mrs. Rossner makes another cup of coffee. She leaves her empty cups all over the house, brown rings pasted inside like open mouths. In the morning Dotty, the maid, will gather them up.

"How about a game of chess?" asks Marshall.

Seung stares. Marshall is planted there, at the door to Aviva's bedroom, with his mauled head, his clear, knowing, innocent eyes.

"All right, one game," agrees Seung.

28

The health club pool is in a vast, high, steamy room, with seven lanes fussily marked SLOW, SLOW/MEDIUM, ME-DIUM/FAST, COMPETITIVE, FAMILY, etc. For now Aviva's mother still has the use of the membership; later, when he gets around to it, her father will revoke it.

The pool is almost empty today. Seung picks one of the slow lanes. Aviva has complained to him that she gets winded easily when swimming, and he promised to observe her and see if he can help. She wears a plain black one-piece that makes her skin look bluish-white. Though vain about her everyday clothing, a lover of the plunging neckline, she dislikes skimpy bikinis and thinks she looks better in something simple and classic. But as usual she cannot risk being invisible, so she keeps her gold hoop earrings on and makes sure she wears waterproof mascara.

She minces about on the shallow-end ladder, oohing and ughing as if she's sticking her toes into dry ice.

"All at once," Seung tells her.

"I never can," she insists. She starts to plunge down, stops helplessly in a crouch above the water. She looks like a toddler about to relieve herself. Seung laughs at her.

"All right," she says, stung, and rolls under. She comes up shouting, shaking like a dog. Her messy ponytail slaps her in the face.

"It's better that way, right?"

"Yes," she says. "But I already knew that."

He tells her she wastes the strength of her arms and legs by rocking from side to side in the water, dispersing her energy. He teaches her to bring her arms up in an arc and push them with intention through the water, in a clean forceful sweep. The legs need hardly to move if they are kept straight and gently tensed. She practices slowly, then moves faster. She can feel the difference.

"My God, it's good," she says. She's exhilarated. For once she feels physically strong, competent.

She does laps until she tires and then sits, warm and satisfied, on the pool edge watching him. He covers the length of the pool in a few hard strokes, curls, and like a circus tumbler reverses direction. By the time he comes out of the somersault he is already halfway back across the pool. His arms are massive as they rise from the water. He swims on and on without flagging. Eventually she goes to her bag for a paperback.

"Will you teach me to do the turns?" she asks, when he's done. He promises. He can teach her dives, too; she just needs a little courage.

The locker room has thick white robes, attendants, face scrubs and scented hand lotions spread out on a long table under illuminated mirrors. Women take their time here, drying their hair, smoothing their skin, watching themselves dress. Aviva and Seung eat triple-decker sandwiches in the club café, order three-dollar lemonade. They sign the bill with a membership number. It will be paid by someone. Aviva's father, Seung assumes.

29

A strange, dry Christmas afternoon. It hasn't snowed since the tenth of the month; on the ground stand the crusty diminished banks of that storm, pocked with dog pee. Seung and Aviva take the bus to her father's new apartment; Marshall is spending the day with their mother. The people out on the streets, passing from one family obligation to another, look bleached and weary. The air is bone-dry; the wreaths and lights lashed to the lampposts shake in the stiff wind off the lake.

Mr. Rossner's new apartment is between Lincoln Park and the Water Tower District, on one of the little streets, dotted with old mansions, where Waspy bankers and heirs to industrial fortunes live. The buildings are substantial-looking, four or six stories high, with manual elevators and doormen in white gloves.

Inside the apartment everything is swathed and draped in heavy fabrics: velvet, chintz, and satin imprinted with flowers, birds, and paisleys. There is some sort of duplication of rooms, or rather everything has the same superfluity of fancy chairs and tables, so that Aviva can't tell which areas are supposed to be for dining and which, perhaps, for guests. Mr. Rossner greets her with a dry kiss and extends his hand to Seung. He leads them to a room with several couches and a large tree decorated with tinsel and glittering balls. There are colorful presents all around the base. The apartment is hot as a greenhouse and smells chemically floral, as if perfume has been sprayed in all the corners.

"There's Edith," her father says.

Edith's hair is wet from the shower and she's panting, as if she ran all the way from upstairs. She's barefoot and in a bathrobe. She has a large painted mouth, large brown eyes, and beautiful skin. Aviva's mother says she comes from a wealthy horseracing family in New York State.

Mr. Rossner is fiddling with the stereo system. It's new and it's been giving him trouble.

"Jews are lousy mechanics," says Edith. Her laugh is staccato, shrill.

"Well, then, my dear, you come over here and mend it," says Mr. Rossner mildly. Edith bends forward and fills her wine goblet, offers some to Seung and Aviva. They clink glasses and talk briefly about their flight from New York and the weather. The wine tastes thick and sweet to Aviva. The heat in the room is astonishing.

Mr. Rossner has got it now: the sound is static-free, the bass adjusted, the music coming from both speakers. It's

Ella Fitzgerald doing Christmas music: "Jingle Bells," "Let It Snow," "Have Yourself a Merry Little Christmas."

"Larry, get us those two shopping bags over there. No, those." Edith points him to two large bags sitting toward the back of the tree. Her hands sport gold and diamonds on several fingers.

Aviva realizes with horror that they have brought no gifts. It didn't occur to her that Christmas here could actually mean gifts. Edith drops the first bag in front of Aviva and the second in front of Seung. "Go!" she trills.

Aviva lifts the topmost box from the bag and pulls at a fat silver ribbon, which slithers to the floor. The box is from I. Magnin; inside is a chocolate-colored cashmere turtleneck. Soft hairs cling to Aviva's fingertips as she strokes it; it's like a sleek, shedding cat.

"Thank you," she murmurs. Seung holds a snow-white polo shirt to his chest, nodding to indicate the size looks right.

"Keep going!" cries Edith. It appears that there are not only the packages in the shopping bags but more presents on the couch for them to open. Edith leaps up to get the boxes, claps her hands wildly whenever she's convinced a gift has been successful. Even when she is still she seems to be in frenetic motion, like a hummingbird whose wings must beat thousands of times a minute just so it can stay in place.

Afterward, the bright wrapping paper lies on the carpet in long, torn strips and crumpled balls. Yards of ribbon, immaculate bows, the hand-cut kind, like huge hydrangeas, that will go straight into the garbage in the morning. Aviva wants to spread all the rich clothes on the floor and admire them, touch them repeatedly. She's also received, among other things, a big box of chocolate cordials, a purse soft as skin from Coach, and two record albums that are clearly her father's contribution: Louis Armstrong and Marian McPartland. Seung got two shirts, a tie, a seersucker sports jacket, two excellent cigars, a sweater, a leather wallet.

The three of them—Aviva, Seung, and Edith—slump back against the couches like people spent after a harsh bout of lovemaking. Edith's long legs sprawl before her and Aviva is afraid that if Edith doesn't sit up, her panties are going to come into view. Or maybe she isn't wearing panties. Mr. Rossner remains upright, sipping parsimoniously from his wineglass. And what is Seung studying at school? he asks after a long silence, as if successfully dredging the sentence from an old phrase book. He's put on one of Aviva's records: Louis Armstrong's low growl fills the room.

Chemistry, Seung tells him. The parents always like to hear chemistry.

Aviva's father doesn't seem to listen. He goes back to squat by the new stereo, lifting his glasses to peer at the lights and dials.

Outside, the lake-blown cold cuts again across Seung and Aviva's naked hands, their unbuttoned coats. They hurry to cover up, to put on their gloves. They are laden with bags filled with things that already feel, to Aviva, tainted and shameful, purloined somehow, and they've eaten all kinds of indescribable things: balls of whipped cheese, nutty something-or-others rolled in bread flakes. At the door Edith told them she was teaching Aviva's father how to enjoy life at last. "All that Jewish earnestness," she said. "It's cute, but so limiting." She laughed her high staccato laugh. Her hand fluttered onto Mr. Rossner's shoulder, her red nails touching his collarbone.

"Don't even tell me what you thought," says Aviva. The cab whisks them down the darkened Outer Drive. Anything human is indoors now, savoring a fire or a TV movie before bed. The lake is a frozen sheet of gray. She leans her head onto Seung's shoulder. There's an enormous pressure in her chest and throat.

"It wasn't so bad," Seung tells her.

"It was worse than I imagined," Aviva says.

30

January classes, the irregular pings and tappings of the radiators, a brief show of sun at midday, the slow seepage of cold into the afternoon classrooms. It's 4:00 PM; the students sit with their peacoats and down jackets draped over their shoulders, frowning at what they've written in their spiral notebooks. Aviva can't concentrate on the lesson. Mr. Lively is explaining something about the Lawrence textile strike of 1912. Aviva read the testimonies in her history book: women struck down with billy clubs, little children thrown in jail cells. For lunch Aviva had a spoonful of peanut butter and a handful of raisins. Coffee of course, three cups. Under the large oval classroom table she rolls around and around in one hand the smooth wooden ball Seung carved for her. When he cut to the core of the wood and polished it to a high sheen, beautiful striations appeared, reddish with glints of brownish gold, like an ore. Last night,

Seung took her out for dinner at the Fisherman's End. They had French onion soup with big hunks of seeded bread. There was a bowl of popcorn on the table from which Aviva ate careful handfuls. Seung brought her wrist to his mouth and licked the oil and salt from her palm.

"Miss Rossner."

Aviva looks up.

"Would you please answer the question?"

Mr. Lively is waiting, not unkindly. He has a boyish face, reddish hair, the sagging skin of a secret drinker. Everyone knows which teachers have the problem. No one suggests it's a weakness; even at fifteen or sixteen years old, they understand. The grown-ups are living on an island of youth here at Auburn, a Never-Never Land. There is nothing for a proper adult to do in this tiny blue-collar town, no theater or art gallery or singles bar or bookstore or park safe to walk in at night. The teachers spend their evenings in their dormitory apartments listening to the sounds of sobbing, scuffling, bathroom retching. The Guignol's last show ends by nine thirty. You could see taking to drink under these circumstances.

"I'm sorry, Mr. Lively, I wasn't paying attention."

Mr. Lively weighs his options. Aviva Rossner is a smart girl, one of his best students in fact, a strong writer, turns in her assignments on time. She makes thoughtful comments in class. She's sufficiently well mannered. Still, lately she's been slipping away. You see this begin to happen with some kids—there's something on their minds, some family business or internal storm, and before you know it they're gone entirely, intellectually speaking, and sometimes they can't come back. They stop seeing why they should. And truth be told there's an arrogance about Aviva Rossner that he's never liked, a sense she conveys of following the rules only because they happen to suit her. Furthermore, she's too sexy, with her snug sweaters, her dangling jewelry. She distracts him.

Another student would have said, "I missed that, Mr. Lively." Or: "I didn't hear." This girl says, "I wasn't paying attention." So sure of her right to be honest.

He gives her an extra paper to write, on the conflict between the UTW and the IWW during the Lawrence strike. Her expression becomes sullen, inward. He's made the right choice. She'll be paying more attention from now on.

31

Those long dim winter afternoons. Neither Cort nor I play a winter sport—Cort used to play basketball but broke his wrist lower year and never quite got his game back afterward. Voss and his wrestling teammate Phil Hurston, who is in McHenry dorm, have a day off from practice. We're sitting in Cort and Voss's room playing blackjack. Phil, a top-heavy kid whose shoulders are way too broad for his waist and hips, likes to be dealer. Why shouldn't he? Odds are in the dealer's favor. I don't care; I don't take this game all that seriously. I engage halfheartedly, thinking about a play I'd like to put on at the Black Box, Auburn's secondary theater. The big productions, like *Macbeth* and *A Streetcar Named Desire*, go on the main stage, and are chosen and overseen by the theater faculty, but anybody can launch a show at the Black Box if they can get the bodies and the slot on its schedule. I'd like to put on a stage version of *The Seventh Seal*. Mr. Boras showed the movie in my History in Film elective earlier this year, and I was deeply stirred by the beauty of the faces—the Knight's, the Squire's, Death's—almost as if Bergman were re-creating stone or marble statues in a moving medium. The acting was grave without being pompous. A whole movie about how desperately we all fear dying! At this time in my life I am drawn, like many young people, to the subject of death—because I have never experienced it close up, don't know anything about it, and believe, foolishly, that I want to know. And of course I like the fact that the characters in the movie who survive the Black Death are the theater people, Bibi Andersson with her full wholesome face and figure, her child-like husband. I think I'd like one day to have such a family, the little naked infant, the simple enjoyment of the sun, the wind, the grass, a bowl of strawberries. Who would be best to play Death, I wonder? I run through my mental Rolodex, dwelling particularly on the counterintuitive choices. Caught up in these considerations, I request a card from Phil Hurston when I should hold, and end up with a ten of spades for my king and seven. Somehow I missed it when the others decided that we were playing for money, and now I'm twenty dollars in the hole, which alarms me. The Judge is stingy and I'm already tight for the month, having blown most of my Christmas money on records and a sweater for Lisa.

Hurston and Voss snicker at my lame play, which gets Cort snickering, too. "What are you dreaming about, honey?" asks Voss in a fey voice. "What's going on in your little hard-on dreams?"

"You still with Lisa *Flood*?" asks Hurston.

I grunt assent.

"She give it up to you yet?" Voss wants to know. "You bust her cherry? Haven't you been working on that for, like, two years?" Once, in a much earlier era, I used to confide in Voss, having yet to learn that anything told to him eventually reached the ears of others.

"You'll be the last one to know, Donald," I say. The guy hates his given name.

"Ooooh, ouch. That was a tough blow, Bennett-Jones. You know how to skewer a guy. That wit. That repartee."

"You hear that Cherie Calkins and Archie Davenport broke up?" Cort can be counted on to steer the conversation when Voss and I get too seriously pissed with each other, which is more and more often these days. I can't figure out why the guy seems to hate me so much. To be honest, I'm not sure we ever really liked each other, but we had the loyalties of long affiliation. We were roommates as preps and lowers, until he got closer to Cort and they asked to room together for upper year, which is how I ended up with David Yee. The two of them and I would probably have fallen out long ago except that we share tastes in music and they like to have me as a third for Frisbee.

"No kidding," says Voss in a suddenly different tone. "You going to go for her?"

"Me?" asks Cort nervously. "I dunno—you interested?"

Voss gives this a moment's thought. "Nah. She's got an annoying laugh." Voss is a good-looking guy, it must be admitted, but he rarely keeps a girlfriend for more than a month. There's always something wrong: her laugh, her eating habits, her friends.

"I'd put up with a horse's neigh for that body," says Hurston.

"Well, you go for her then," says Voss.

"Just might."

Hurston deals the cards again. I get a king and a five. Bloody hell.

Some music goes on upstairs.

"Oh, Jesus, that whiny shit," says Voss. It's Seung or one of his friends, sounds like maybe Chick Corea accompanied by irritating flute. That laid-back, electronically trippy, life-is-cool sound is one that all of us particularly hate.

"Christ, I can't take it. Bennett-Jones, put something on." I'm only too happy to comply. I reach for Devo on Cort's album rack, crank it up. *Yeah yeah yeah yeah, yeah-yeah-yeah-yeah-yeah-yeah*, intones Mark Mothersbaugh a million times, singing of urges and purges and losing control. The harsh, repetitive, jerky music draws us together, pumps us up with a sort of manic-robot gladness. We wave our fists around and shout for our cards and I am not surprised when I get a six of hearts for my fifteen, earning back the money I just lost.

A banging noise on the ceiling: Seung or one of his buddies with a broom handle, probably. In reply we raise the volume. After a few moments of silence upstairs, in which we are tempted to believe we have settled this skirmish, there's a startling explosion, which seems to be the result of three or four sets of hands simultaneously overturning desks and beds and sending a lamp crashing to the floor. Once the surprise passes, I'm delighted. I start jumping up and down, shouting at the top of my lungs, grinning at Cort and Hurston to encourage them, and they catch on and start jumping up and down, too, and then Voss has to follow suit, and we all thrash around wildly screaming "*Are we not men? We are Devo!*" over the music. Cort runs to get his hiking boots from the closet and throws them repeatedly at the wall. Voss and Hurston and I get the rest of the shoes and follow suit. We throw them at the wall and at each other, shouting and cursing, drowning out the presences above.

A loud knock. Any good idea at Auburn always ends up like this. We all knew that from the start.

It's not Mr. Glass but Mr. Leonov, another resident faculty member, less mild-mannered than Glass is. He's short and brutally muscular, and I wouldn't be surprised if even at his age, which seems to be around fifty, he could still take on a guy like Voss.

"Turn off the damn turntable and sit down on your beds and shut your mouths," is all he says. We do that in exactly that order, and when it's quiet we realize that it's quiet upstairs also. A calm quiet, an easygoing quiet, with some movement and light banter in it, not our scorched-earth, chastised silence. You can always tell the difference. While we were acting like maniacs Seung and his band must have righted the beds and the desks and sat down like little angels, maybe commenced testing each other on German conjugations. Mr. Leonov walked right past them and came to us. How stupid could we have been?

"All four of you are on restrictions," Mr. Leonov says. "One month." Voss and Hurston groan. I silently curse; the evenings would have been my time to court actors and start rehearsing for my *Seventh Seal*. A month of eight o'clock check-in kills my plan pretty thoroughly; by the beginning of March kids will be looking ahead to the big spring play or spring sports and won't want to tie up their time. And there will be the note that goes home to my parents. Just what I need. Cort looks genuinely chagrined, as if he'd like to apologize for doing wrong; I want to slap him and tell him to get some balls.

When Mr. Leonov is gone, Voss turns to me. "You're an idiot," he says. "What's wrong with you?"

I don't even bother to answer, to make the obvious retort that he was jumping up and down and yelling his head off just like the rest of us. Because he's right. I'm an idiot. My heart fills with an astonishing hatred: for Voss, for Cort, for big lopsided Phil Hurston, for Mr. Leonov and Seung and Detweiler and Giddings and Sterne. For my father and my mother. For my two brothers and my roommate and every teacher I've ever had at this damn school and my coaches and the fat ticket-taker at the Guignol, the change makers at the Rexall, the operators who hook me up for my forced monthly collect call home. For Voss's imperfect girlfriends and the pretty untouchable babes on campus and the ugly undesirable ones and Lisa Flood. For Aviva, who belongs to Seung. For myself, naturally, above everyone.

32

Now we trudge back from the library or the gym or town every evening at 8:00 PM, even on Saturdays; Hurston has to cancel a planned trip to Boston. We hardly speak to each other, each blaming the rest for his predicament. I try to use the time to study, to improve my grades in math and science, but my concentration isn't good. I stock up on Snickers bars and Twizzlers. Good thing I'm not doing crew this spring.

Two weeks into restrictions the weather warms, just to make us really regret our confinement. Fortunately, the daytime is still free for all to enjoy. The air lightens and there's a breeze smelling of earth and river water. The sky is a whitish blue. I feel a cheerfulness in spite of myself, and wear shorts under my blazer and tie. The girls are out in peasant skirts—tiered, floaty things—and sandals. It is maybe fifty-five, sixty degrees. Every January or February there's a run of two or three days like this, freakishly temperate, then the season remembers itself and blows bitterly again.

Cort and Voss and I toss a Frisbee. When it suits him, Voss has a thoroughgoing amnesia about the enmity that has passed between us, and Frisbee frankly makes me whorish, I can never resist an invitation. I am very good at the game; it's rare that I can't run the disc down, and today, as I fly across the lawn in front of Weld, leaping and diving, never, somehow, fumbling a catch, I find myself imagining that Aviva is watching, seeing and marveling at this physical grace that I have only, it seems, at these moments, and only when I do this one thing. It's such a beautiful happening, so odd and unfamiliar, to be out on this mid-February afternoon, that it makes me hope for fantasies to come true.

All the same I know that Aviva can't be anywhere nearby. She and Seung will have gone to the woods with a knapsack containing a blanket, a cheap tablecloth, a bottle of wine. There will be other couples out there, too, but the woods are spacious, there is room for them all. Carlyle and Gene Murchie are there. Gene crumples Carlyle's pants into a thick ball, wedges his wild head between her legs. If you take a walk along the creek, you can see the empty rum and whiskey bottles, dirty condoms, sometimes a sock, a lighter, an old pencil. They must have such contempt for the act of love, the couples who leave such things behind. Even their cries of pleasure they must see as pollutants. Aviva and Seung never leave anything behind, I'm sure of it. They fold the tablecloth and the blanket. They fit the bottle, not empty, back into the rucksack. Aviva checks her earrings, her necklaces. Seung runs his hand through the grasses just in case. They walk slowly back onto the athletic fields, not sorry about anything.

Carlyle doesn't join the girls for dinner. Perhaps she's gone to the library or is rehearsing for chorus. But Lena and Aviva are concerned. They worry about her. She's like a big overgrown child, they think: plump, healthy, and much too good-natured. She gets herself into trouble trusting people, encouraging people, offering her help.

They discover her in bed, knees drawn up, reading *The Thorn Birds*. She's wearing her nightgown and a big floppy hat. They all know immediately what has happened. They climb onto her bed, push themselves close. Even Dorota is silent, ceding her usual place at the center of a narrative. Carlyle raises her head and removes the hat. Her left cheek is a deep reddish purple. The purple seems dusted with silvery highlights, as if a painter went back and wanted to add something mystical to the composition.

"At least he didn't get the eye," says Carlyle.

Yes, for chrissakes, she tells them, she put ice on it, do they think she's stupid? She puts her fingertips to the spot. Dorota says to let her have a go at it. She's going to spread Noxema on it. She swears it heals everything.

They minister to her on the bed, three girls in nightgowns, smelling of toothpaste and Wella Balsam and soap. They have young, soft hands. They dream up violent and humiliating punishments for the wrongdoer, but they don't speak them now. This time is worse than ever before, this time Gene has crossed the line. And Carlyle mustn't listen to his poison, the way he makes her believe that she is to blame. Carlyle shakes her head. If they only knew, she says, if they could only understand how selfish she is, how thoughtless.

"Even if that were true it doesn't give him the right . . ." says Aviva.

Carlyle fixes them with a look of impatience. Why doesn't anyone really listen to her? The swelling makes her left eye look smaller than the other one. "Not just selfish, not just thoughtless . . ." She trails off. She can't put words to the knowledge inside, the knowledge of what is wrong with her.

"Please," pleads Lena. "Break up with him. We'll help you."

Carlyle nods, wipes her nose with the back of her hand. She'll listen for a night, two nights, she'll make promises, then they'll lose her to him again.

33

Seung's letters embarrass Aviva. He slips them into her knapsack, leaves them in a cubby on top of her hat and mittens while she eats her meal in the dining hall. She sees the tiny, spiky black handwriting on the envelope, her name surrounded by oceans of white space, and a depression takes her. He cannot use the English language. It is simply true. His sentences are stiff and exalted, filled with abstractions. He has been "struck by a lightning bolt." The experience of being with her "fills his veins with fire." His words irritate and upset her. She has never felt these things he has felt. She often longs for Seung, she relies on him, but her heart has not been pierced with a deadly arrow. Under no circumstances would she die for him. She had a pen pal once, years ago; they found each other through a pen pal service at *Teen* magazine. The other girl sent a photograph of herself. She had teased blond hair and the look of small-town enthusiasms. She wrote that she was in love with Donny Osmond. *Real love*, she wrote. *Not just one of those crushes*. What had the pen pal girl's name been? Oh, yes, Sherri. With an *i*, and the *i* dotted with a circle.

On a sunny, snowy Sunday, I leave my room on the third floor of Weld. I don't remember now where I was going, perhaps just out to get some air. When I reach the second-floor landing, a figure moves toward me from the direction of Sterne and Seung's room, a girl, small, a blue scarf around her neck, snow boots up to her knees. I remember that the drawstrings on the boots were untied.

Surprised, I stop where I am and let Aviva go by. I smile. She catches my eye but I can see she isn't frightened. I'm nobody. I became nobody to her a long time ago. She has a protector now, a boy who's as good as a man. He'll never let anything bad happen to her. There's no way, she thinks, that I could come between her and her pleasures.

She moves quickly and quietly down the stairs. Clearly she's done this plenty of times before. Sterne holds the front door open, but his raised hand halts her for a moment. He looks out once again, in, out. "Go," he orders.

When she's gone, Sterne walks up to meet me. I haven't moved. He walks slow, rolling from the hips, so I'll be able to feel, in my breadbasket, his long muscles, how tight and strong and sudden they are. He moves across the tennis court like a panther. His backhand is his best stroke. And now I notice that someone else is near me: Detweiler, who must have been the day's second-floor sentry, looking abashed. He'd waved Aviva on before he heard me approaching. Seung, I imagine, is still in his room, running a towel under his armpits, pulling on a fresh shirt.

Sterne finishes his slow ascent and comes up close to my face, very close. It's just like a movie. "You say anything to anyone and we'll paint your freak flag with your sorry brains," he says.

"Oh . . . no," I say, still smiling absurdly. This pathetic tatter is all I can get to come out of me. If I had another minute, perhaps I could pull myself together, draw myself up and say something more dignified. *It's cool, Sterne.* Or: *Don't get your knickers in a twist, man.*

"No, you won't say anything, or no, you're not sure, and I should go ahead and bust your skull open?" Sterne wants to draw this out, to force me to take a role in my humiliation.

I keep smiling, smiling, cursing myself. "Why would I say anything?" I ask.

34

What I do next:

I turn back toward my room, Sterne's eyes still on me. I lock my door, not that anybody would be likely to visit, but I need to be able to put such a possibility out of my mind. I know David's still in Boston on an overnight he took to visit a cousin.

I get into bed, pull the sheet lightly over me. If for some strange reason David did return I could roll over in an instant, say I feel sick, I threw up, I was sleeping. I reach under my boxers, but the first image that flares up in my mind is the butt of my hand knocking Sterne sharply under the chin, his smile crumpling and his teeth flying out of his mouth the way they've flown out of mine in certain terrible dreams I've had. I'm hard before I'm even conscious of thinking about Aviva. But here she is now, as my hand moves up and down; she's riding on top of me, moving slow and deliberate and then gradually faster, hitching a little on that sensitive spot at the top that she knows is so right. I think that for once she's actually going to stay. It's strange, but although she often sends me here, into my bed, under this sheet, she always dissolves almost immediately into something else, one of the generic bodies that have served my purpose since I first figured out what jerking off was all about. I try to keep her, literally slow the mental film so that I am approaching her obscured figure from behind, turning her to me, pushing her gently onto my cot—gently, I repeat, so as not to scare her, so as to show her that I won't be idiotic and clumsy the way I was at the boathouse. It never works: she becomes yet another creature with long, straight blond hair, featureless skin, a large mouth, big smooth haunches. Nothing like Aviva.

But now Aviva towers above me, as if to say all right, I can have her, but she is going to be the one in charge. Okay, okay, I silently agree, thrusting up to the rhythm of my fist, but the faster I go and the closer I get, the more my mental Aviva slows down and withholds herself, telling me to wait, I'm just going to have to wait. I don't want to wait; I push against her, calling her bitch, saying filthy things. She bends way over me then, pinning my hands to the mattress, her hair all over my face, getting in my mouth, blinding me. She laughs like she laughed that first day I met her, in her room, a laugh of encouragement and maddening aloofness. I start to beg: *Please, let me go, let me come, let me,* and in a whirl of motion that shatters her image and makes her disappear yet again, she does.

35

Cynthia Pritchard asks, "Is this short story saying that love, for a girl, is like being murdered?"

The whole class laughs, but when the laughter dies down, there's a long ripple of discomfort. Cynthia is always so earnest, so anxious, so embarrassingly undefended. Silence. Mr. Salter can hear all the girls thinking rapidly, restlessly, and no one wanting to answer. He jumps in, hoping to save the thread. "Cynthia, can you walk us through how the author might be suggesting this?"

The story they're discussing is "Where Are You Going, Where Have You Been?" by Joyce Carol Oates. It appears in their fat anthology, *Explorations in Fiction*. In it, a fifteen-year-old girl named Connie, home alone while her family is on a picnic, is visited by a mysterious and menacing man who eventually, hypnotically, persuades her to get into his car and drive away with him.

Cynthia fixes her eyes on the text and speaks slowly, her voice a bit strained.

"Well, at the beginning, Oates takes all this time to talk about how flirty Connie is, how she dresses up and wants to meet boys, and how alienated she feels from her family. Like, she's *looking* for someone to take her away from everything. But then, when someone comes to do just that, this Arnold Friend guy, and talks about being her lover and holding her tight, you know that if she goes with him, she's going to end up dead. So it's almost like the writer is saying that when you're female, if you fall in love, it's, well, the end of you."

"So," says Mr. Salter. "You are reading the story not literally but as a metaphor?"

Cynthia exhales. "I guess," she says.

Mr. Salter opens his arms in invitation to the class. "How did others of you read it?"

"I think you're reaching too far," says one of the boys. "I think the girl gets stalked and then kidnapped by a psycho and that's the story Joyce Carol Oates wanted to tell. She's just trying to write a suspense story."

"The guy's name is Arnold *Friend*," another girl points out. "That can't be an accident."

"Are we so sure she's going to die at the end?" asks Aviva Rossner. "I mean, it doesn't *say* that."

"It's almost like she's going into some sort of dreamland," says a third girl. The boys have been conspicuously reticent during this conversation. "Maybe we're not supposed to read this so realistically. I mean, this Arnold guy is sort of supernatural. He knows all about Connie's family and her past and even what she thinks about. Maybe he's just supposed to represent the inside of her mind, how she realizes she's growing up and needs to leave her family but is scared to leave her family. Like here—page 376—Arnold says, 'The place where you came from ain't there anymore.'"

"That's sort of what I was trying to say," says Cynthia fretfully. "Right after that part, Arnold Friend says the house Connie lives in—'your daddy's house,' he says—is so flimsy he could just knock it down if he wanted. Like, she can't stay a little girl anymore, but if she goes with him she's lost, too. He says, 'Be nice to me, be sweet like you can because what else is there for a girl like you but to be sweet and pretty and give in?'"

"This is one of the scariest stories I've ever read," offers a girl named Jill Cohen.

"I was going to talk about point of view issues," says Mr. Salter, giving a slap to *Explorations in Fiction*, "but Cynthia has gotten us onto an interesting line of thought. Can we think of other ways in which the stories in this anthology have depicted sexuality between girls and boys, or men and women?"

The class comes to attention: the girls sit up straight in their chairs, the boys press their knees together. Mr. Salter didn't use the evasive trick word *love*, he said *sex*.

"Ummm . . ." says Frank Corbitt loudly, breaking the tension. Everyone titters.

"What about in 'The Dead'? Or John Cheever's 'The Five-Forty-Eight'?"

"I'm drawing a blank," says Frank pertly.

"I surrender," says Mr. Salter finally. "Think about it on your own, then. And some of you, if you're interested, might want to take a look at a book by Erich Fromm called *The Art of Loving*. There are some striking ideas there about love and sexuality. It might deepen your reading of this and other stories."

Later, in the library, Aviva hunts furtively in the card catalog, hunched over so no one else can see the cards. *The Art of Loving* turns out to be a slim paperback with a hot-pink cover, and Aviva skims through it wondering if she has the guts to hand it over to Mrs. Conn-Frere, the librarian, to be checked out. She decides she does. She pulls other books off the nearby shelves: *Psychoanalytic Approaches to Love, Love & Death: An Existentialist Exploration*, a volume merely called *Intimacy*. When she gets to the front desk she'll tell herself she's writing a research paper on the psychology of love. She'll believe it for the one and a half minutes she needs to get the books stamped.

For now she takes a carrel and begins to read, keeping the pink book nestled unobtrusively in her lap.

> The deepest need of man, then, is the need to overcome his separateness, to leave the prison of his aloneness . . .

Yes! Aviva thinks. Yes! When she goes for a bathroom break she places the little book, and the one called *Intimacy*, under the more sober-sounding *Psychoanalytic Approaches*, turns all three volumes facedown, and shoves their spines against the back of the carrel where they won't be readily seen. But Cort, working nearby, uses the opportunity to check out her reading, and reports back to Voss and me that Seung Jung's chippie apparently does some research to amplify her bedroom skills. We enjoy this tale greatly for a couple of days—at least I pretend to—but aren't bold enough to pass it on; it might get traced back to the source.

Aviva takes the books to Mrs. Conn-Frere, gazes into the distance as she's checked out, and over the next two days she reads *The Art of Loving* as often as she can, taking notes in her rounded handwriting on loose-leaf paper. She reads only when alone in the room and is careful not to leave the notes on her desk where her roommate might see them. There are passages in the book on that terrifying term, *frigidity*. Is she, Aviva, frigid? A woman, writes Fromm, "opens the gates to her feminine center; in the act of receiving, she gives. If she is incapable of this act of giving, if she can only receive, she is frigid." Does this apply to her? Is the reason why Seung can never enter her that she only wants to receive from him and not give? Why does the book not talk about the thing that has happened to Seung and her; why does no book ever talk about it? It is unique, unheard-of—that's why.

Love is active, the book tells her. Love is giving. Love puts the other person's needs above one's own. The woman is receiving and the man is penetrating.

For several days Aviva feels hopeful: Fromm has told her what love must be and, with her student's sense of purpose, she will follow the guidelines and emerge with success. She will love Seung properly and something will subtly soften in her without endangering her or making her afraid. Seung will sense that new softness, that womanliness; he will come in. Aviva attempts to think of Seung's needs, which she can hardly even picture. He wants to please his parents, even if, behind their backs, he acts the scapegrace. Other than that, he seems simply to need to be with her—her, Aviva. She wills herself to love him for himself, not simply because he loves her so blindly—but what is "himself" besides this blind lover? She doesn't, in fact, care about his schoolwork, the nitty-gritty of his home life, his childhood memories, his plans for the future. Or not very much.

The little book, inspiring at first, becomes a scold. She will never be able to live up to it, she doesn't even understand it. "Immature love says: 'I love you because I need you.' Mature love says: 'I need you because I love you.'" How can one possibly sort this out? How can Aviva even imagine a love so ideal, so disinterested? She returns the book to the library, along with the others she took out that day, which she has not bothered to open, and as they fall down the slot in the front desk, she feels a great relief.

36

When our month of restrictions is finished, I'm not quite sure what to do with myself in the evenings. I feel slow, fat, and blinkered—a confused mole. The first night, I wander around campus, resisting my desire to go to Currie's for a milkshake; besides, I don't want to sit alone. Voss has been acting again as if restrictions was all my fault, and whither goes Voss goes Cort. So I'm on my own tonight, unless I want to hang out with David Yee in the library and talk about partial differential equations. I should make some new friends. Yeah, right. My time in this place is almost over; I'm just looking to ride out the final months and make a new start next year, somewhere far away. Somewhere out of the reach of my father, somewhere I will start to be whatever it is I think I'm capable of becoming.

I walk in the direction of the Dramat, not that anything is going on there tonight, but it soothes me just to be nearby.

The spring production is *The Playboy of the Western World*, and I'll be props master, but tryouts aren't for another week. When I pass the Academy church, I hear singing coming from within. I keep walking, but the notes trail me and pull me back. The voices are very sweet, and maybe I want to be in a room filled with people rather than alone in a darkened theater. I make my way in, standing at the back, not yet committed to a seat and a stay.

It's the choral choir. They have a surprisingly good turnout; perhaps there are others besides me who feel at loose ends on this chilly, interseason evening. I see Aviva in the pews—my eye always finds her instantly in a crowd—and next to her are Lena Joannou and Kelly Finch. They are gazing up at the stage, all attention, and I see that their friend Carlyle Johns is one of the singers. The bright lights on the pulpit are distorting, but something about Carlyle's face looks wrong, as if she fell down and bruised herself. My eyes slide to the other faces, boys and girls, all lit up, mouths open, static yet shifting like the faces I imagined I would put in my production of *The Seventh Seal*. They are wholly fixed on their task and move in perfect unison. So preoccupied am I with watching that for a while I don't even hear any sound, I'm aware only of these sculptural faces. Then the voices return, with a purity that surprises and unbalances me, and something shifts painfully around my heart. It's only the girls singing now, and their voices are so high and sweet; if I were at all religious I would think they were lifting me up somewhere closer to . . . what? Something radiant and uncorrupted. After a few moments the male voices come in again, enriching the range, rumbling but still pure, and I have to sit, my legs won't hold me. I push my way into a spot in a back pew, receiving a look of annoyance from a girl I don't know, and once I'm there I'm so shaken I can't look at the pulpit anymore. I drop my head and close my eyes. The music keeps coming and I know I've made a mistake; I don't want to hear this beauty, which won't stop but pushes at me relentlessly. It's too much; it threatens to hurt me. I'm tempted to cover my ears but manage to sit on my hands to keep them still, squeeze my eyes tighter, and bear it. I should have known not to come into a room where everyone is leaning in as one, everyone is feeling as one. I'm not meant for such places. I ball my fists. It will be over soon, I keep telling myself. I try not to hear the beautiful music. Soon it will be over.

37

Seung's parents are in Boston for a research conference Mr. Jung is attending, and Seung takes the bus from Auburn to meet them at their hotel. He has something to tell them. He isn't asking for permission. He's already paid the deposit for two nights at the beach cabin on Nantucket; the money is his own, saved from his lifeguarding job. He's decided— naturally he doesn't say this—that he and Aviva need to go away somewhere, far from the ducking and hiding at school and the parental shadows at home, in order to succeed in their physical union. In a new, bare place he'll be able to give Aviva what she seems so to need; he will be virile and whole. For a while, the two of them were able to be happy deferring the inevitable but lately he can tell she is thinking about it again, wondering, growing agitated. And he? He doesn't know what he feels, what he wants. But there's a vibe in the air, and it makes him jittery. Aviva is slipping from him, he senses it; or is he making things up? Sometimes when they are together her attention seems far away; there is something she is pondering that makes him as envious and frightened as he would be of another lover.

Two nights and three days in Wauwinet, Seung tells his parents, and then he'll come straight home for the rest of the April holiday.

His mother says very well, then, if he is such a man, if he makes the decisions around here, then she and his father will stop paying for his Auburn education. He can come home and get a job and go to public school. She says that he thinks he is a man but he is just a little—she uses the Korean word for shit. Seung's father says nothing, which makes Seung know there is a chance everything will be all right. He watches the chopping motions of his mother's hands as she appeals to his father in Korean. She grabs her purse and leaves the hotel room. Then Mr. Jung pours two glasses of whiskey from a bottle in the minibar and says that he does not approve of this little Jewish girl, he thinks her spoiled, lacking in propriety and good sense. She will be bad for Seung in the end. But he can see, he says, that Seung has the fire in his belly for her, and there is nothing to be done about that. He will have to let the fire burn itself out.

"Just don't do anything idiotic. You know what I am saying. And do not think, for a moment, of marrying her. You are way too young and it would be a great mistake."

Seung grabs his father by the shoulders, almost hugging him, and his father embraces him. They are both overwhelmed by this gesture, and they stand for a long moment before parting.

38

One day Giddings returns to his room after lunch to find Detweiler still in bed. He is sitting on the mattress with his legs crossed as if he is planning to meditate. Pillows are propped between his back and the wall. He wears flannel pajama bottoms and a once-white T-shirt with holes in it. His head swings slowly toward the door as Giddings enters.

"You cut classes, man?" Giddings asks.

Detweiler smiles, that sweet, slow smile they all know him for.

"No," he says. "It's just that I can't leave the room."

"Say what?" Giddings replaces his morning books in the bookshelf and selects his afternoon ones.

Detweiler doesn't answer, just smiles.

"No shit, you really haven't been out?" But Giddings can see he hasn't been.

"I know it's only a short distance between this bed and that door," says Detweiler. "And now the door is even open.

So I should be able to do it. I should be able to stand up and put my clothes on and walk in that direction. Even if I didn't take my books and didn't brush my teeth, it would still be a good thing. But from here it looks very, very far. The door just looks far."

Giddings thinks Detweiler has been toking, a stupid thing to do right here in the room. "You stand up with me," he says. "I'll help you get dressed, and we'll walk together to the door."

"No," says Detweiler. "No. I have to do it myself and I just haven't been able to. I'm sure it will work itself out eventually."

At three o'clock, Giddings comes back to check on Detweiler, this time with Seung. Detweiler hasn't moved from the bed, but now he is crying quietly. "I don't think I'm crazy," he says. "I know I'm me. I'm Jeremy Lawrence Detweiler. My mother is Susan and my father is Anthony. And that's you, Giddings and you, Jung. I was supposed to be at calculus for first period and I've got cross-country in half an hour. I know that there shouldn't be any problem standing up and walking across the room."

It takes four of them to carry Detweiler down the two flights of stairs and into the ambulance that pulls onto the lawn outside Weld early that evening: Seung, Giddings, Sterne, and Mr. Glass. Before calling Mr. Glass the three boys make sure there aren't any drugs in Detweiler's system. "Not even coffee," Detweiler insists. Later Dr. Van Neelan comes over from the infirmary with Ms. Merton, one of the psychology counselors. Detweiler's parents in Michigan are contacted and agree to have him moved to Peter Bent Brigham in Boston.

There is a stretcher waiting behind the ambulance but when Detweiler sees it he panics and tries to twist free, demanding to be put down. He can sit just fine in the vehicle, he begs, there's no need. They confer with their eyes, then set Detweiler on his two long legs, whereupon he climbs into the back of the ambulance very calmly. They see him reach for his seat belt. They've managed to get him into a pair of jeans and a pullover. "It was just that thing of getting out the door," he reassures them.

"Don't worry," he continues, as the ambulance driver restarts the engine. "I'm not *totally* all right, but I'm not crazy. I'm pretty sure I'm not. I mean, I don't believe I'm Jesus Christ or anything."

39

The college envelopes arrive in the mailboxes, fat and thin. I never did fill out my application for Dartmouth. I had plenty of money in a fund from when my Aunt Marcie died, and when my father blew his gasket, as he surely would, I'd just tell him, in essence, screw you. I didn't even think he'd hit me. Both he and I were getting a little old for that sort of thing.

Once the word goes around, kids are mobbing the PO, pushing to get to their boxes. I retrieve three skinny envelopes and one thick, solid one. It's from Bard, which is my first choice. As soon as I've muscled my way back out of the room and reread, with pleasure, my letter of acceptance, my mind turns to Lisa. She will certainly have gotten into either Yale or Brown, most likely both. A few weeks more of school, and then I won't be seeing her again. I feel doubly lightened.

Seung is accepted at Colgate and at Rutgers, his safety school. That evening, he phones home. There is a silence on the other end. Mr. Jung had hoped for Harvard.

"Dad," Seung says. "I'm a reasonably intelligent kid who tries hard. I'm not Harvard material. You know that by now."

Dak-ho Jung begs to differ. He points out various bad decisions Seung has made—taking advanced drawing instead of physics II his upper year, messing around with his school band instead of keeping up his classical music studies—but his heart isn't really in it. "Harvard is the best," he says at last. "Auburn is the best, and you should go from there to the college that is the best."

"C-Colgate is a good school."

"It's the girl," his father says, and now he sounds more sincere. "You waste all of your time on that girl. You're infected, it's like typhus with you. She's made you frivolous. You think only about pleasure."

"It's not true," says Seung grimly. If only his father knew.

40

A blue hand has been spread over the sky; the sun throws warm patches on the walks. We can smell it, the coming of spring. The trees are barely budded, and the air is still very cold. But the turning has arrived, it's unmistakable.

Sterne says it's time for the Spring Jubilee. No one has ever heard of the Spring Jubilee. It's never been celebrated before. That doesn't matter. They all agree to behave as if it is an ancient Auburn tradition, passed down by the sons of clergymen to the sons of industrialists to the sons of the intellectual meritocracy. They, the boys of Weld, are the latest in a long line of votaries paying homage to the Lady Spring.

They are full of busyness all at once, roused from their winter apathy. Sterne reminds them that the signal ritual of the Spring Jubilee is the making and drinking of mint juleps. He produces a pint bottle of bourbon from the winter boot collection. Giddings is dispatched on his bicycle for sugar and shaved ice and mint. He returns to report that the grocer has explained that mint is not in season until June.

"Of course it's not," says Sterne. "Did you get the Wrigley's Spearmint Gum?"

"Oh, for fuck's sake, Sterne."

"In the Spring Jubilee, Wrigley's Spearmint is always used as a substitute for fresh mint, due to mint not yet being in season."

Giddings takes off again. In the meantime, the Grateful Dead lands on the stereo: "Shakedown Street," "Good Lovin'."

Urban Engelsted, a kid they sometimes hang out with, brings out his shot glass collection, and Seung lines up the little glasses on the windowsill. In the room now are Seung, Sterne, Giddings, Engelsted, and Engelsted's buddy Mark Dasgupta. They are all aware of a space that would have been occupied, quietly and inwardly, by Detweiler. Every couple of months, there's some casualty, someone you know who is expelled or fails out or cracks up. This winter it was Detweiler. Spend long enough at this school and you can do a roll call of disappearances, tally the little score marks on your heart. Sterne puts a stick of gum in the bottom of each glass and adds two spoonfuls of sugar. With the long end of the spoon he mashes the gum and sugar together. "We call this bruising the mint," he says. "The technique was developed back on my old Kentucky plantation, before it was destroyed by carpetbaggers. Do not remove the wad of chewing gum; it is considered impolite. But do not swallow it."

The sound of clinking glasses, cold hands high-fiving.
Young men are sprawled in chairs, their knees spread.
Someone—Giddings?—has found a lei left over from a vacation, a theater production, who knows what. He drapes it
over Sterne's chest. The Grateful Dead segues into Jackson
Browne. They toss back the shots and refill their glasses,
not bothering about the sugar or the gum. A bolt of late-
afternoon sun enters the room, illuminates Sterne where
he sits like the May King. Giddings has stuck an unbudded
magnolia branch in Sterne's hair. All five boys daydream,
lost in secrets it is all right not to share.

Seung is the first to leap up at the knock on the door.
Sterne has the glasses collected in an instant, shoved into
a pillowcase. He's noiseless and fast. Giddings nudges two
empty pint bottles under the couch with his heel.

It's Mr. Glass. The music is a little loud, he says. His eyes
move around the room, landing on one boy after another,
on the bookcases, the desks, the window sill.

"Oh," says Seung, "sorry about that. We thought we were
being quiet."

Mr. Glass laces his fingers together, allows the silence to
lengthen.

"Would you like to come in, sir?" Seung asks.

"Not really. No, I would not like to come in. I would not
like to have to come in. Do you think you get my meaning?"

"I think so, sir. I'm sure we don't want to give you any
reason to have to come in."

"All right, then. You're a proctor, Seung, remember."

"Yes, sir."

He's gone.

Nothing can spoil the Spring Jubilee. In one afternoon, in one incarnation, it's become an authentic ritual, which is to say it is something that's become necessary, non-negotiable. They won't ever forget. The true rituals have the habit of escaping, of finding those who will perpetuate them, and so next year, somehow, someone will know about the Wrigley's gum and the bourbon, will circle on the calendar the date exactly eighteen days after the spring solstice. In five years, some of the older alumni will believe they have memories of commemorating the Spring Jubilee themselves. The Jubilee will make its way into yearbooks and the graffiti on basement walls.

Sterne stretches out on the couch, his body lit up by the setting sun. Giddings hums a hymn sung in chapel every Tuesday and Thursday morning, a hymn that, as he doesn't go to chapel, he didn't know he knew. Seung closes his eyes. For long passages of the afternoon he has forgotten Aviva. When he drinks, he can sometimes forget her. When he smokes reefer or drops acid, he only feels her presence all the more, lit up in pulsing colors, more pressing in her physicality, her strange, rebuffing need.

We all felt the spring coming. I went down to Voss's room, to see if he'd come toss a Frisbee with me. He never locked his door, I walked right in as always. He looked up at me from the couch. Cort's back was to me. Voss's hand lay on Cort's shoulder and his jeans were unzipped. He didn't seem as if he quite saw me. His mouth was swollen. "Ah, Christ, Voss," I said. The number of ways there are to be left out, to be abandoned. I backed out of the room, shut them in again with their privacy.

41

A Sunday afternoon. Aviva and Lena borrow two bikes and head to Starport Beach, about eight miles from Auburn. It's a tricky trip that starts along the busy state road with Water-lilies, the Chinese restaurant, and McDonald's and Friend-ly's, hits the highway for a while, then gradually veers off onto the boulevard that passes along the shoreline, with its newly re-awakened motels and fish shacks and sportsmen's dens. Aviva and Lena sit on an Auburn-issued bed blanket, sweater arms pulled low over their wrists, smoking Lena's clove cigarettes and looking across the bay at the marshlands where a big power company wants to build a nuclear plant. Mr. Lively has told them about the letter-writing campaigns to stop the construction and the violent protest rally that was held in Starport last month. Aviva pictures the squat tubular forms that may rise on this land, sending their in-visible damage, their cell-warping frequencies, out into the water lapping the beach and the homes nearby.

"I'm going to die a virgin," moans Lena.

"Enough of that," says Aviva. Sometimes it's annoying, always having to tell Lena what she wants to hear. "You will not."

"Easy for you to say."

Lena has brought *Wuthering Heights* with her. It's one of her favorites; she's read it six times. Aviva borrowed it from her once but found Heathcliff repellent, Catherine incomprehensible. The characters gnashed their teeth, shrieked, struck their heads on hard objects until they bled. Everyone sneered and was agitated. Aviva doesn't understand what Lena finds so compelling.

"It's the way Heathcliff can't think about anything but her," says Lena. "The way he would rather be damned to hell—and they really believed in hell back then—than be separated from her."

"I wouldn't want him to think about me even for a minute," says Aviva. "Him and those dogs? Please."

They are silent for a while. Aviva is always on guard against the possibility that Lena will ask her what it's like with Seung, how it's different when your virginity is gone. In the butt room, for months now, she has smiled and kept quiet while the others talked about boys, sex, kisses, asses. The others think it is the smile of knowledge, the silence of wisdom, and leave her be.

Lena's current crush is Calvin Arthur. He's the best pianist on campus, tall, good-looking, and black, or as the kids are learning to say now, African American. She and Calvin have gotten friendly at the music building during the long hours they both spend practicing there. They're working on a Schubert duet they plan to perform in a school concert.

"It's hopeless," says Lena. "He'll never have a white girlfriend."

Aviva demurs. Why should that matter? But they both know it does. Most of the black kids sit at all-black tables in the dining hall, have their own dances, their own clubs, listen to different music, care about different movies. Lena says you have to look at things through their eyes. There are only a handful of black students on campus. Calvin tells Lena that she can't imagine how different are the worlds from which they come.

"He went to a fancy private school in Delaware!" protests Aviva.

"Calvin says it doesn't matter. If you're black, you're treated like ghetto, and you get to be a little ghetto."

"He's just trying to talk himself out of you, because he's scared," says Aviva. "Stay with it. Don't give up." She sounds idiotic to herself, dispensing romantic advice.

Lena hands her a banana. "You're looking really scrawny," she says.

"I'm 105 pounds, like always," says Aviva. But she actually doesn't know how much she weighs. She hasn't gotten on a scale in months. She doesn't want to see how much space she takes up.

They grow quiet, watching the water, listening to some early birds. Aviva gnaws unenthusiastically at the banana and then puts it aside. Lena opens her novel. Aviva's brought a novel, too, but lately she has trouble reading. She can concentrate enough to get the sense out of the books and articles she reads for school, but thinking with any clarity takes twice as much time and effort as it used to. She opens her knapsack. On the first two pages of her book she becomes bewildered by what seems like a great deal of dull detail about train times, coats, mufflers. She starts from the beginning and tries again. Her attention slides off the page. She tries to revive it by turning to the back cover and reading what others have said about how great this novel is. It's a slim book, and there are not that many words to a page. It's incredible that she should have this much trouble staying interested.

"I'll tell you what would have happened if Heathcliff had married Catherine," Aviva says, causing Lena to look up. "He would have started beating her. You think he would have done that only to Isabella? Catherine Heathcliff, abused woman. *But, Heathcliff, we're one, I'm you, you're me, more than myself*, blah blah. Eventually Catherine poisons his dogs and him, too. The end."

"God, Aviva!" cries Lena.

"Don't listen to me, I'm just in a crappy mood," says Aviva.

42

The first thing my mother does when she meets me at the train is tell me she's made me her meatloaf. Her meatloaf is one of the few recipes she knows how to make since mostly the maid cooks—Jean. Jean still comes five days a week, even with Andy and Dan and me gone. But my mother has it in her head that her meatloaf is something I was wild about when I was a kid, that I was always asking for it. I don't remember this, but who knows, maybe it's true. Anyway, she makes this meatloaf for me at moments of special emotion or celebration, and spring break seems to qualify doubly this year. One, I am home (although there have been other school vacations when she seemed hardly to notice that fact), and, two, my grades have finally improved, although too late to be of use on my college applications. (The Judge wrote a six-word reply to my letter informing him that I did not get into Dartmouth and in fact hadn't applied there. It said, *You are making a serious mistake.* I had to admire his restraint.)

The other news my mother offers is that Andy is home "for a little while." Her eyes flicker anxiously into mine, a signal to ask no more.

My mother's meatloaf tastes perfectly good. I don't mind eating it. As usual, she serves it with roasted potatoes and a big bowl of applesauce. My father isn't joining us for dinner; he has some sort of meeting with a local muckety-muck. He's thinking of running for the state legislature.

"He just can't stand to see the corruption and incompetence anymore," says my mother. She runs her finger under her pearl choker.

"I'm sure he'll get everything cleaned up lickety-split," says Andy. His long legs are sprawled under the table. He's practically lying down in his chair. He's eleven years older than I am. Dan, who's between us, is twenty-four and lives out in Columbus, Ohio.

"Absolutely," says my mother, missing, or deciding to ignore, Andy's irony. "When your father puts his mind to a thing . . ."

Andy tosses back his chair so fast it goes skittering into the corner. I watch it spin perilously close to the curio cabinet with our parents' wedding crystal: the clock, salt and pepper shakers, ashtrays, bears and giraffes and elephants. Andy makes a lot of noise going upstairs. His plate is full. I've never seen him like this. He's always been Andy: my much older brother, handsome, competent, happy, full of minor devilry and good nature.

"What's the matter with him?" I ask.

"I don't think he slept well last night. It's amazing how cranky that can make a person."

For dessert my mother offers large scoops of ice cream slathered in Hershey's sauce, a childhood specialty that I am, in fact, often nostalgic for. Afterward I knock on Andy's door.

He's lying in bed, listening to something on one of those new Walkmans. He sits up and pulls off the headphones.

"Sorry, bud," he said. "I just can't stand listening to all that shit about Dad anymore."

I can't believe it. Andy was always the good son, despite the low-key mischief he used to get into. He took the summer jobs the Judge wanted him to take. He went to Dartmouth the way he was supposed to. He and the Judge used to stay up talking politics late into the night. The Judge adores Katy, the woman Andy married.

"What are you doing home? What's going on with Katy?"

He crosses his legs primly. "Marriage is a for-shit idea. Katy's been porking some other guy."

"No!"

"Yes."

This is beyond imagining. Andy still has that lock of dark hair falling over his forehead, the one that made all the girls in his year fawn on him and vote him Most Wanted in the school yearbook. Even a younger brother can see that he's a damn good-looking son of a bitch, and the way his face has thinned out, gained a couple of lines around the mouth, only enhances his appearance. He's twenty-nine and athletic and funny and from everything I've been able to see, he's a good dad. What could Katy be thinking? Can my brother be right about her?

"I've thought about killing the guy," Andy says.

His face frightens me. "You're not serious, are you?"

Andy sits up straighter. When this was his room, there was a rough wool blanket on the bed. My mother's replaced it with a quilt made up of triangles with pink roses. "For a while I thought I was. Now I'm not so sure. I know how I'd work it, though. I had it all planned out. I was going to take Katy for a ride, tell her we were going out for dinner, and instead stop at Prickhead's house. Have her ring the doorbell. Tell her to get back in the damn car. Then, when Prickhead comes out, run my Ford Torino right onto his front walk and mow him down. Let Katy feel the crunch of his bones under the wheels."

He speaks with so much relish that I can't even look at him. I just keep my mouth shut and hope he's not crazy enough to think this would be a good idea.

"Don't listen to a fucking thing Dad says," he finally tells me. "Don't major in what he tells you to major in, don't marry the girl he wants you to marry, don't take whatever job he thinks you should take."

"I'm already pretty well down that route."

"Well, good. Because he doesn't know a fucking thing." I notice Andy hasn't taken his shoes off. He's scuffing at the quilt with one dirty toe. He's going to tear the quilt. I feel bad about this, for my mother's sake, but not bad enough to say anything.

"So I'm not going back," he tells me. "Katy wants her new life, Katy gets her new life. She always was focused on her own big self."

"What do you mean, not going back? What about Gil?" Gil is Andy's three-year-old. I've only seen him three or four times. Andy and Katy live in northern Maine, where Katy's from. Much as he was in favor of Katy, my father always has some excuse not to travel up there. Once they had the baby I think he knew he couldn't just walk in and act like the boss of the place; Andy and Katy had a new authority.

Andy finally takes off the damn shoe and tosses it on the floor. Then the other one—thud. "I hate being apart from Gil," he says quietly. "And abandoning a kid is about the worst thing a person can do. But I can't explain it; I just can't go back and hang around the edges of that dopey little town, where everybody knows what's happened, that I'm the big cuckold. I can't just tie the whole rest of my life to that nothing place, and her, and her parents, when she's the one that did wrong." He rubs his eyes, hard, the way I used to see him do when he was up late studying for an important exam. His grades were never that terrific. The Judge got him into Dartmouth through some sort of hanky-panky, I'm sure of it. Dan was always the one who stood out at school.

"Do you mean you're, like, never going to see him or Katy again?"

"Maybe. Maybe I'll go to Texas, or Kuwait. When did you become such a force for the moral good?"

"I just think it would be hard for, you know, Gil."

Andy leaps up and starts pawing through the shirts he's hung up in the closet, like he's thinking of packing up and taking off again. "Tell me something I don't already know."

There's a soft tapping at the door, which I left slightly open when I came in. I can see my mother standing behind it.

"Are you comfy in here, Andy?" she asks. "Do you need a fresh washcloth?"

Andy stops rattling the shirt hangers. "I'm fine, Mom. Thanks a lot. I have everything I need."

She steps inside the door. "I got you a few more wash-cloths," she says. She's holding a stack of six or so from the odds-and-ends closet: lavender, sea-foam green, tan, white, all the superseded shades of her bathroom color schemes. She's clearly a little drunk already. She holds the stack out with two hands.

"Thanks, Mom. Sorry about the mess in here. I'll clean it up tomorrow."

"Oh, don't worry about that. Jean will take care of it. She takes care of everything. I wonder what time your father will be home?"

"Don't wait up for him, Mom," I say. "You know he can be really late."

"Yes, that's true," she agrees.

Later that night I hear her fall. I'm asleep on top of the covers with a Nietzsche handout lying on my chest. My eyes open in the dark. Andy is fast asleep. I've always been able to hear that—people sleeping. When I was a kid I could tell you if my mother was way under or just fitfully dozing. Her fall makes a truly heavy sound, the sound of something drained of all buoyancy. I can tell she's in her bedroom, at least, not on the stairs. I keep listening. It takes a while, but eventually I hear feet again, her groping around the furnishings in her room. My father's absence fills the house, except for that one heavy space my mother is taking up. I won't go to see if she needs help; it would only give her one more shame to have to misremember, to hide.

43

Seung has bought a ring for Aviva, a thin gold band with three tiny, diamond-shaped rubies in a row. She needs to have something on her finger when they check in at the beach house. It will be good too for when they go out in the little town. Aviva looks at it uneasily. A ring like this costs something. She wants to know where he got it.

"That's my little secret."

"Did you sell drugs for it?"

"It looked just like you. I knew it was the one for you."

"I don't want to take it if that's how you got it."

"I didn't say that's how I got it."

He lifts her hand and slides the ring onto her finger. It is like the moment in the wedding in front of the rabbi or the priest. As soon as it comes to rest she feels she has made Seung some sort of promise. She spreads her fingers to look. The ring makes her small, thin hand look womanly, dressed. It's a beautiful ring.

"Like they'll believe we're really married," says Aviva.

Seung borrows a friend's car, a Mercury Capri. He drives smoothly, and for Aviva's sake more slowly than he likes. Otherwise, she'll press her hand nervously against the dashboard as if she is protecting them from a crash. She makes little squeaks when they round a tight curve. The woman at the manager's hut hands them a key off an oaktag board without a second look. Their cabin is weathered and lopsided, but inside, the pine paneling is new, the kitchen gleams. They put away the groceries. Seung has brought a chicken, which he plans to roast slowly with fresh cherries, dried apricots, and a sweet white wine. He's brought pasta, too, and tomatoes and herbs for making a sauce. He learned how to do the sauce from Sterne, who has an Italian grandmother. Seung picks up something from everybody. He assembles himself from those around him.

He's brought cognac. He's brought whole coffee beans and an electric grinder.

They go out to walk along the beach. The wind is up, and Aviva huddles in her down coat, a scarf around her nose and mouth. She breathes her own hot breath. Seung is never cold; heat streams off him. He wears a duffle, the hood down, the toggles unfastened. They squat in the sand. The sky is yellow-white; you can just make out the outlines of some clouds. Aviva nestles her back against Seung's belly. He draws his coat around her with one hand, with the other he holds a book that he reads to her. It's titled *The Truth Behind Famous Phenomena*. Seung has a weakness for the

occult. The book says that the Bermuda Triangle is a pro-
jection of rage. The angry dead of the native tribes of southern Florida and the Caribbean, abused and slaughtered by
the white man, concentrated their energies into creating a
force field of destruction between his ports in Miami, Bermuda, and Puerto Rico.

"Oh, come on, Seung."

"Don't dismiss it. There are physical and psychological
dynamics we can't possibly understand."

He believes in UFOs, in an afterlife in which he will meet
and hash out old differences with his loved ones and rivals.
He will never truly be dead, he says. Crystals may have
power, and there are certain frequencies that can be picked
up from inanimate objects. Omens exist. The ring was a
good omen, the way it called out to him from the jeweler's
in Back Bay, then fit Aviva's finger exactly, settled on her like
a fragment she had been missing. More often there are bad
omens. He has the sense, at times, of something malevolent
approaching him, growing closer by the month. He doesn't
know what it is.

Inside his coat Aviva is warm. Her shivers subside. She
unlaces her sneakers, pulls off her socks, and plunges her
toes into the cold sand. She traces her name, clumsily, with
her big toe. Then, annoyed with herself for not thinking of
Seung's name first, she rubs hers out and writes that instead.

Back at the cabin Seung builds a fire. He finds a metal
bowl among the kitchen things and puts out flour, sugar, a
bag of chocolate chips.

"What now?" Aviva asks anxiously. Sweets, peanut butter, the tin filled with sugar in Auburn's dining hall: they
fill her now with dread and longing. She no longer trusts
herself. At times she worries that if she starts to eat she will
never stop.

Brownies, Seung says. Hash brownies. He has the world's
best recipe.

"Well. Maybe. Just a little."

She's had pot twice before. Once she and Carlyle and
Dorota went out to the football field and passed a joint
Dorota had. How had Dorota come to have it? Aviva did
not ask. All these purchases and connections—Aviva has
no idea how they work, who meets whom and how. Afterward, for a long time, she thought she felt nothing, but on
the walk back to Hiram the ground tipped up to meet her.
She was climbing a great hill, although she did not grow
winded. The landscape seemed to be stretching to meet the
sky. By the time they reached the dorm, the world had settled down flat again. She thought perhaps she had imagined
the change, brought it on through wishing.

The other occasion was nearly a year ago, before Auburn, with Marshall. He brought home a joint wrapped in
a scrap of paper towel and asked her if she wanted to give
it a try. She could tell it was a new thing for him, too. Some
kid had given it to him, he said, in exchange for his help
with math homework. He didn't really want it but would
feel bad to waste it. They chose a night when their parents
were at the symphony and sat in Marshall's room amid his

skateboarding paraphernalia. Nothing happened. Perhaps altered consciousness was a myth, like the myth of love, that myth that made you write that your veins were filled with fire and that you would die without et cetera.

"Thatta girl."

They kiss as the room warms and fills with the rich smell of chocolate. Seung feeds Aviva little chunks of warm brownie. She nips his fingers.

"Do you think one brownie is enough?" she asks. "I want to feel something this time."

"You should have more."

She eats another one. *I am getting dreamy*, she thinks. *I'm getting calm, happy. Or something.* Seung runs a bath; he wants to wash her hair. She closes her eyes as she slips into the water, like a child who feels invisible when she can't see. Her nipples are buzzy, sentient. She stretches out and lets her head go under the water. Warmth bathes her eyes and cheeks, and her ears fill with murmurs. It's true: even in a bathtub fed by pipes from municipal waterworks, from urban plants, you can hear the ocean. Her hair floats away from her in long ropes.

Aviva's hair is like a sack of coins in Seung's hands: heavy, heavy. He works the shampoo through the coils, combing with his fingers, tugging gently against the knots. He presses her scalp with his fingertips, improvising a massage. He makes her rinse and then starts with the conditioner. The suds join around her, hiding her naked body from view.

"You have to leave it in for five minutes," she tells him. She has coarse, difficult hair; it takes the stuff time to penetrate.

While they wait he sings her a tune, beating out time on the rim of the tub. The goose bumps come up on her arms as the warmth slowly leaches from the water. When she's all rinsed out, Seung wraps her in one of the large worn towels the rental agency has provided, and combs out her hair. Then he discards the damp towel and wraps her in another, dry one.

"I'm not feeling anything," she complains. For a while she thought she was, but she isn't. She eats two more of the brownies. Seung's had six already, seven.

She lies on her belly on the couch, the towel lightly covering her waist and buttocks. Seung's shirt and jeans are unbuttoned. He begins to massage her neck. He presses the small of her back and the burning sensation there brings tears to her eyes. It is as if he's found an extra storehouse of pain, hidden away like outdated munitions, and is emptying it. She begins to cry in earnest now. "I'm not sad," she says. He presses his lips to her neck, kisses her from the knob where her neck meets her shoulders vertebra by vertebra down to the coccyx. He says it: *coccyx*. Another scientific word he likes. On the way back up he uses his tongue instead. He turns her over and continues on her neck, breasts, belly. He gets up to drink a glass of water. Aviva begins to shake all over; she has grown very cold, every pore feels open. A cold wind is pouring through her without cease. She forgets Seung for a time; she doesn't know how long. She is not aware of thinking. When she begins to surface again she has the sensation of having taken up residence somewhere else entirely. She sees before her a great maze, with endless branching pathways. She knows precisely what has happened: she has been transported to the inside of her own skull, and the pathways she sees are the pathways of her own brain. She calls out to Seung, alarmed. She seems to be moving along these pathways, not in a bodily way but as some other form of presence. She is following corridors, some wide and some narrow, with a sense of burrowing farther and farther away from the outside, the outside where she can stand and look at herself, see a head, shoulders, legs. She is inside, and so she can't see anything. She thinks she may become lost, that she will forget how to make her way back.

Seung is right there, next to her, asking her what is it. He's been there all along. His shirt is off; she remembers pressing one cheek and then the other against the smooth surface of his skin. She explains as best she can. She knows, she says, that she's on the couch, in the cabin. Suddenly that seems obvious; there's nothing to worry about. She asks him what time it is. One thirty in the afternoon. "That's good," she tells him. It's another bit of data anchoring her to the world. But she knows that if she relaxes her vigilance she will slip inside the maze again. There is an inside and an outside to thoughts, and to be utterly inside them means dissolution. She feels herself moving down the corridors again. She grabs Seung's arm, calls to him to hold her. But even the warmth of his body doesn't draw her fully back.

It's an anxiety reaction, he tells her. There's nothing dangerous in the stuff. He's with her, he says, nothing is going to happen to her.

The walls of the maze are high, golden, glowing. She cannot see above or beyond them. She pleads with Seung, but she can't hear her own words.

He takes her by the hand and walks her to the bedroom, where he thinks she will be more relaxed, and where he can easily lie next to her. He draws the covers down, gets in beside her, spoons himself behind her. He cradles her head in his hands. She must just relax, he tells her. She is here, the hundred pounds of her, in the bed with him. There is no inside to get lost in. She has an outside as well as an inside. His statements are contradictory but they all seem sufficiently true.

She is quiet at moments, calmly forgetful, and then she remembers her fear and stiffens, breathes shallowly, cries out to him to help her leave the maze, help her get *outside*, please, please . . .

"Talk to me, talk to me," she begs.

Seung curses himself. This brittle, fragile girl; he should have known better. He is careless, careless, an idiot entrusted with a jewel. How could he have let this happen? He himself loves to disappear, loves being drowned in the wash of shapes and lights and extravagant thoughts, being not himself anymore but part of something Other, even when that Other is brutal and menacing. The exquisite relief of not being himself, or any individual at all. But he should have known that for her, Aviva, it would be different. Her needs and her nightmares are so wrapped up in each other that it is impossible to disentangle them. She has told him in so many ways that she fears the loss of control. How could he have ignored this? His duty now is to hold her for all the hours to come, hold her fast, cooperating with her delusion if that's what's necessary, riding the panic out.

"Don't let me slip away . . ."

He talks to her, he tells her that of course he won't let her slip away; as long as she holds on to some part of his body she can't go anywhere, see? A lie, of course, because he knows people who have slipped away—Detweiler, for just one—but you have to make a bridge of lies for the other person to climb back on. She holds on to him and for minutes at a time his flesh makes her safe. Then she doubts it, the power of that flesh, and begins to whimper, to call out that it's happening, it's happening again, she's starting to become lost. He talks to her again, puts her hand on a different part of his body. *Leg. Thigh. Neck.* Until somehow the solidity of this or that part convinces her. They just have to run down the clock. It will be a long, long afternoon.

A little after five Aviva falls asleep, exhausted, her lips dry and her eyes fluttering beneath the lids. Seung waits awhile, then steals to the bathroom and wipes his face and neck and underarms with cold water. He sits by her side with a glass of water. On the nightstand lie a pencil and a pad of paper, a small amenity of the cabin, and he takes the point of the pencil and drives it into his thigh until mere physical pain is transformed into a deep bodily objection. He holds the self-made blade there ten seconds, twenty, then slowly withdraws it. What kind of lover is he, to force on her these kinds of adventures? She wasn't made for them.

At five forty Aviva wakes with a start, looks around. "Math class," she murmurs. Precalculus, with Mr. Singh, it starts at five forty.

Over Seung's protests she struggles into her clothes, runs her fingers through her still-damp hair. Her balance is off; she's clumsy tying her sneakers. He'll run her down on the beach if he has to. At the bedroom door she pauses, looks at him.

"Oh, God," she says.

She comes back to bed. He can feel her humiliation. He puts his hand on her shoulder but she pushes it off. He strips off his jeans, no longer needing to be dressed, to create that makeshift authority for her benefit, and once again lies next to her, leaving space between them. He spreads his hand over his hard penis. Not here, not now, he chides himself. The chicken he bought sits in the refrigerator, fresh and trussed. The apricots and cherries are plump and good. It's still not too late to cook. He has a vision of candlelight, of cognac winking in the glasses and the smells of stewing fruits and broth with wine. There is still something good, something hopeful to be done with the evening. He rises again and pulls on his boxers, a T-shirt. He pours himself a glass of wine, then with deliberation he chooses the pans, bowls, knives he needs. He lays out the cutting boards, looks at them with satisfaction. There is something for him to do. Aviva will sleep again, and then she will feel better. When she's ready to join him, he'll sit her down, make her comfortable, give her a glass of warm milk.

44

The next day the heavens open. A driving rain all day, so that they cannot go out. The moist cold seeps in through the gaps in the cabin's frame and settles in Aviva's bones. She wears an oversized wool sweater of Seung's, her hands balled inside the sleeves. She still doesn't feel quite right. Her skin is a fragile covering; when she closes her eyes she sees cross-hatching, a faded and reduced symbol of the golden maze that almost had her trapped and lost forever. Her concentration is shot and she can't even read a magazine. She wants to do nothing but sit by the fire and warm herself as best she can.

The rooms are still filled with the smell of the meal Seung made last night. Aviva couldn't eat it, so Seung packed it up and they had it for breakfast at eight and again at noon. Seung plays cassette tapes he's recorded for her: Jean-Luc Ponty, Jean-Pierre Rampal, Rachmaninoff's Concerto Number 2.

He plays the concerto's piano part on her back, and for the first time rouses in her a laugh. Their mouths meet. The continuous tropism of their hands toward each other. They break, woozily, watching the fire, and Seung draws a cougar for her with the short, thread-thin lines he favors. The eyes appear, like precision-cut jewels; the spots are distinct as puzzle pieces, no two exactly the same. He uses the sides of his colored pencils to shade in reds, mauves. He has captured something in this animal: it is not quite realistic, and yet it is alive, like an animal in a dream or a fable. Aviva can see it stir on the page. Its eyes are eyes to be frightened of. Seung signs his initials in the lower-right corner in tiny lettering, along with the date: 4-23-80.

The fire flickers low in the grate. Aviva's palms fill with Seung's smooth and taut places, her legs twine with his. He is very hard against her and she reaches down to wrap her fingers around him. He spasms in surprise and they quiver apart momentarily. They are too earnest to smile. Aviva sidles closer again. He moans from someplace deep inside that knows emptiness and expects never to be filled. His fingers move to her thighs; she parts them, suddenly afraid. The languid warm feeling drains away; she watches warily as he feeds himself into her. He cannot fail, she warns herself and him simultaneously. He won't fail. She grows very still, waiting for him, absenting herself a little, in order to make this his work, his burden. She doesn't want to be mocked again. She can't let herself want this too much. Does Seung feel that slight withdrawal, that implicit challenge from her? He nudges past the outer lips; his mass, his density, make her flesh feel dense in return: more real, more present. Whatever else she has felt in this field between her legs has been abstract by comparison: mere vibration, music, rather than solidity, sculpture. He pushes a little farther and she cries out in both arousal and anxiety. She had pictured this entry always as a sliding and a melting, a dissolve into pure sensation. It is duller and more physical than that. She does not know if there is pleasure in it. There is heat and a burning. It is happening, it is happening. But just as she is adjusting to these perceptions she feels him diminish; though he insists, he no longer advances. She pushes herself against him to help, at first energetically but soon without spirit, suspecting there is no point. And there is no point. She wants to shout at him to stop, not to shame himself by butting at her and prolonging the failure, but he goes on and on until she puts her hand against his chest and shoves him away. He does not even raise his head to look at her. He expresses no surprise. He curls up in fetal position, his fists hidden under his belly. Rage radiates from his hot skin.

"It's all right, it's all right," she lies, folding herself around him. He shakes violently; she can hear and feel his teeth chatter. He tries to speak to her but stutters so badly that she can't understand what he is saying. Whatever cassette was last playing clicked off long ago; the rain thrashes heavily on the roof. Aviva's arms ache, stretched across his broad back. She knows she should speak to him as he spoke to her when she was lost in her altered world: make soothing noises, reassure him, stroke his back and shoulders. These are all things that a kind and good person would do. But she can only stomach the one brief lie. She is bound to her sense of honesty as if to a whipping post.

There is something within her, she is certain, that creates damage. The horror is that she cannot control it. And Seung too tells the truth, merely in a different way than she does. Just as she will not lie with her mouth he is unable to lie with his cock.

45

Seung's mother does not greet him with a smile at the train station. They make the short trip home in silence. Seung's father is not yet home from work, and the entire house seems to accuse Seung with its emptiness. As if, even though he has returned, he can no longer be resident here. He does not fill up its space.

His mother retreats to the kitchen, to scour and bang. Eventually Seung is compelled to go out. He walks toward the main commercial street in town; maybe he'll check out the five and dime. Or maybe he'll keep on as far as the park, sit and watch the little kids on the slides and swings. There is a light, misty rain falling, not enough to keep the children away. It brushes pleasantly against his face. He sticks out his tongue to see if he can catch the drops.

When he gets to Jordan Avenue, all the shop doors seem to rebuff him. He isn't wanted here, either. He walks until the shops peter out and the streets turn residential again. The maples are fully leaved and there are tightly budded tulips beginning to show on the lawns. He recognizes the dog before he recognizes the girl. The dog's name comes to him instantly: it's Pebbles. Pebbles is a beagle, tan and white, with large soft eyes. The girl went to school with him at Jordan Middle. She was a big girl, with soft round shoulders, large breasts, a pleasant face, pretty but a bit heavy. A nice, friendly girl. Not in many of his classes, the top-tracked classes. Not stupid, but not in that tier. Jill—Seung has it now. She's slimmed up some, lost the glasses; she looks easy in her big body, confident, matured.

She waves to him from down the block, calls his name. As he draws close he feels it—the vibration these home girls used to give off. Different somehow from the vibe that goes round at Auburn: a little more forthright, a little needier. Even back in middle school, when he was still Chinaboy, he got the vibe from plenty of girls. He was the kid who ran the 440, who could execute a complicated twist off the board at the town pool. The girls would gather in twos and threes, wanting to talk to him. Why did he never capitalize on this? He was fourteen, for chrissakes—that's why. In the afternoons and evenings there were track practice, piano practice, and Mom and Dad wanting to see you hitting the books. But he'd known the vibration, the desire, was out there. He'd planned to claim it in time.

He remembers the dog because Jill used to walk it around the park while his team was having track practice. Now he wonders if that merging of schedules was really just a coincidence. The dog would get inspired by the runners and charge along the lanes in pursuit, exhaust itself after a loop, and lie down whimpering like a diva in an extended death scene. Jill would stand with her hands on her hips and laugh at the poor thing, then scoop it up in her arms and scold it affectionately. The team called the pooch, a female, Jessie, for Jesse Owens.

Seung and Jill stand together in the drizzle, Pebbles yipping and jumping—like a pup, still—around Seung's feet, tangling him in the leash.

Jill throws her arms around Seung in a hug, as if they'd been good friends in the way back when. "It's great to see you," she says, asking if he still goes to Auburn. She has a good memory, he tells her.

"Oh, no," she says. "I mean . . . you were memorable."

She is wearing a hooded windbreaker but the hood is not up. The rain sifts down on her nose and cheeks, her eyelids. There is thick mascara on her lashes and a hint of blue on her lids. The dog is very wet but does not seem to mind. Jill lets go of the leash to let it play in the puddles. It rolls in the cold water, waving its paws around frantically.

"Filthy dog," she says.

Jill too is on vacation, she tells Seung. Or really she should say that it's her parents who are on vacation. They went into the city, to stay at a hotel and take in some museums and theater. She stayed back to watch over Pebbles. She hates to board her. And really she doesn't mind. She prefers the company of Pebbles to looking at bunches of old paintings.

"Do you want to come in for hot chocolate or something?"

Her house is not far. She disappears into a bathroom to peel off her wet clothes and emerges in a thick white bathrobe. The door to the bathroom remains open and he can see the soggy jeans she has discarded. She's combed out her hair, and for some reason this stirs him: the smooth, even grooves running the length of the shaft. She's wiped away her mascara and now looks fresher, younger—younger than Aviva, even though she's not. Her generous breasts are visibly bare beneath the robe.

"We could make that hot chocolate," she says.

"That's okay," he tells her.

In response she seats herself on the bed, waiting, and he realizes that she means to watch him undress. With Aviva, he is always pressed up so close that he cannot see himself, his own nakedness. They are always touching or so close to touching that there is no space for looking. Seung quickly removes his shirt, then unzips his jeans more slowly. Jill scoots back against the headboard and unties her robe. She spreads the folds back to reveal herself fully. When Aviva does let him look, she turns her eyes away, as if to remove herself from her vulnerability. And he cannot remember ever having the sensation that she has looked at him entirely, complete, not in pieces: an arm, his chest, his cock. He feels weak in the knees, in this room of Jill's with posters of Cheap Trick and Blondie and the stuffed animals propped on her dresser and nightstand. In a moment, he is on top of her. It goes so fast. He can't help himself. Perhaps he kisses her once or twice, maybe his hands graze her breasts. He is inside her before he knows it. She inhales sharply. He knows it's all wrong, he's come into her too soon. It's boorish, inelegant. He can't help it, can't help it. He tries to compensate by brushing his hand against her hair, pressing quick kisses against her forehead, but it's too late. He groans, pushing frantically, and comes in several long spasms that seem to last longer than everything that has come before. He is wet from head to toe with sweat and excitement. He stays inside her for a long time, silently thanking her, praising her, apologizing to her. Perhaps she will not despise him, if he lies here like this and holds her for a while.

After a while she wriggles beneath him, signaling that his weight has become too much. She sits up. "Well," she says.

"I'm sorry," he says. "That was . . . I just lost my head."

She shrugs, tips her head to one side. A beautiful, forgiving girl. An angel. "Again," she says. "Just let me go put in more goop."

She slips into the bathroom. There's the sound of a drawer opening, a short blast of water.

This time he slides in slowly, gently, only after kissing and stroking her breasts and thighs, the soft hollow of her collarbone, murmuring sincere endearments about her hair, her lips, the way she feels. She sighs and shifts to bring him in deeper. He is amazed at the grace they achieve, the way they pass pleasure back and forth between them like the intake and outflow of breath. Her exhales grow longer, deeper, louder, and then she clutches him tightly, her nails pricking him, and he can actually feel the muscles inside her spasm around his cock. He has been languid and cool this time around, but now he suddenly seizes and spills into her. He shouts out without knowing it.

They shower together and, as grateful as he is to her, as happy as she seems, he can hardly bear the minutes until he can dress and leave. Her nakedness now seems too much, a feast that has gone on too long, a picture of excess. He is afraid he will try to take her again in this stall, the door smeared with steam. The hot water floods down on them in endless eruptions. He fucked her the first time for his honor, the second time for her pleasure. The third time would be the crime.

As he slips on the wet shoes he left at her front door, the loafers he wears when he comes home from Auburn so that his mother will not ask, *What do they teach you up there, to wear dirty sneakers?*, he reminds himself that the whole time he hardly gave Jill his mouth, nor took hers. That would have been a greater betrayal of Aviva than his cock inside this girl has been. Jill's cunt could never feel as dark to him, as mysterious, as Aviva's mouth when she opens it to him. He could never fall as deeply inside.

Jill takes her coat from the coatrack and puts a hand on his sleeve. "Let's go out and get something to eat," she says.

He is a gentleman. They go to the diner, order hamburgers, root beer. He listens to her talk about the girls' soccer team, the tickets she has to a Fleetwood Mac concert. He pays the bill and walks her home.

46

Aviva can see the difference that just four months have made. The tide of money that always washed in without pause, without even being noted, has permanently withdrawn. The maid, Dotty, no longer lives in. Mrs. Rossner says she comes twice a week; it was necessary to cut back. There are dishes in the sink waiting for a scrubbing. The grout in the tiled kitchen countertop is sticky and discolored. The cookies in the cookie bin taste stale, as if her mother has felt it too much of an indulgence to replace them, although her economies could hardly extend this far. Mrs. Rossner mentions that she's given up the box at the symphony. "I called the box office and gave it back before your father could get it in the settlement," she says. "There's a wait list of ten, twelve years for one of those now. My one small act of revenge." She smiles her wintry smile.

Marshall is at school all day; he already had his spring vacation. Aviva plans to rise early each morning and walk

him to the bus stop, but when her alarm clock goes off she
feels a brutalizing heaviness that makes her turn over and
sleep again. She stays in bed until eleven o'clock, sometimes
noon, then goes to walk along Clark Street, looking at the
shops. The weather is sunny and brisk and helps her waken
at last. She buys herself a late breakfast at the Parthenon
Diner, even though her bank account at school is running
low and she is afraid her father will not send her May allow-
ance on time. Last month he was ten days late. She stops in
the little stores where she used to spend her pocket money
on dangling earrings, embossed pencils, decorated mugs,
stuff that seems like junk now. Some of the salespeople are
the same as always and they greet her.

On her second day home, Aviva walks into a hair salon
that has a cleanly swept window and artful head shots at the
front and asks a hairdresser who's free to give her a short
cut. The woman takes three steps back, studying, then
comes forward to heft Aviva's curls in one hand. She lets
them fall. "Are you sure?" she asks.

Aviva is sure.

The woman gives her magazines to look at, asking her to
choose a picture. "This would be cute," she says. A young
woman is seen in profile, the tips of her dark hair, which
reach no lower than her earlobes, plastered against her cheek.

"All right," Aviva agrees.

It causes some notice in the salon. Other customers comment on the long black ropes on the floor.

"Well, it's more modern," says one.

"You should save a lock," offers an elderly woman. She produces a Baggie from her purse.

Aviva watches herself in all the shop windows as she walks home. She appears, disappears, appears again. She likes the haircut. Her head looks sleek and clean. She looks like someone who cuts to the chase, who doesn't overthink or waste time. She smiles at herself and catches the smile in profile. People are watching her move down the block with such certainty, such intention.

"Whoa!" Marshall shouts when he arrives home from school. Suddenly Aviva doubts herself.

"What do you think?"

"Whoa *whoa!*"

"That bad?"

"No! You look like a model. Only you made such a big deal when I shaved my head."

"Well, you did a terrible job."

"It's better now, isn't it?" he asks anxiously. His hair has pretty much grown back in, although unevenly, and is for some reason darker than before.

"Much."

"Why did you do it?" he wants to know.

"Why did you shave your head?"

They look at each other.

"Will Seung like it?" Marshall asks her.

"I don't care what Seung likes."

The hunger that she flew home with is gone and she can no longer eat her meals. The cereals and biscuits in the pantry make her mouth go chalky. Now that Dotty isn't around there is little fresh food and no cooked dinners. Mrs. Rossner catches meals on the fly—a bowl of cereal, peanut butter on crackers—or forgets. In the evenings Aviva makes herself and Marshall scrambled eggs or tuna fish sandwiches. They go out one afternoon and stock up on a few things at the supermarket. But most of what they throw together she can't put in her mouth.

Their mother is emptying cabinets, going through old boxes shoved to the back of closets. It's an ominous sign. Is she planning to move? "Look what I found," she says. She is not a woman prone to nostalgia, yet once upon a time she apparently took the trouble to fix black-and-white family photographs to an album with sturdy black pages. The photographs are held in place with little white corners, but many fall loose when Aviva turns the sheets, their backs stained yellow with old glue.

Their father is almost absent from the photographs, as if all that time ago he already anticipated his disappearance. Of course that is nonsense. It is because he was the one taking the pictures. Their mother looks slim and severe, more European than she does now. America has smoothed her out, created a bit of slack in her face and posture. Marshall is a chubby boy with full cheeks and various expressions of inward delight. He seems never completely present, but his absence is benevolent, fond. Aviva appears as the responsible older sister, her hand on Marshall's shoulder turning him toward the camera, or sitting with him on the rug holding up the flash cards she's made, large capitals in thick marker, to teach him how to read.

A couple of days later, after Aviva washes her hair, the cut doesn't look as sleek and sculptural as it did at the salon. The hairdresser did something special with the blow-dryer and some gel. Aviva can't replicate it. Her hair stands away from her head, bushy, dull-looking. She ties one of her mother's silk scarves around it and that's better. But later she takes it off. She tells herself her hair looks fine the way it is.

Marshall will turn thirteen the week after Aviva returns to school, so they have a small celebration, with cupcakes Aviva bakes but cannot manage to eat. Marshall says now that he's going to be a teenager he will become responsible and good all the time. He will do all his work and be interested in his classes. Mrs. Rossner says that is wonderful news if true. Marshall is going to summer school after all, to do catch-up work in English and social studies especially. No summer baseball for him this year. For a gift, Mrs. Rossner has bought Marshall an enormous book of baseball statistics, which makes him leap around with delight. Aviva, with careful budgeting, was able to buy him a Walkman. Surprised, awed, he throws his arms around her.

They sing a round of "Happy Birthday" for Aviva, too. Her birthday is not long after Marshall's, on the sixth of May, and she won't be home until June. Marshall says he'll send her present in the mail, once he figures out what it is. In the past he's given her a painted snail shell, three of his beloved Plastic Man comic books, a poem with stanzas praising her best qualities, one for each year of her life, and, back when collecting these was the center of his existence, a package of Matchbox cars.

A few days before the end of Aviva's vacation, she and Marshall make a trip downtown to see their father. Edith is on a visit to her sister's in New Jersey, but the apartment is still magically filled with the scent of her perfume. Although Aviva and Marshall have not mentioned their mother, Mr. Rossner announces that he prefers not to talk about her, now or in the future. It was time for things to come to an end, that's all. He'll always be there for them. He takes them to the enclosed pool on the roof. The air is cold under the glass dome but the water is supposedly heated. There's a lifeguard with floppy blond hair who crouches alertly over the vacant pool, ready to address any misfortune. Muscled, anchored, he looks maybe twenty or twenty-one. Someone masculine and competent who can't be bothered with college. Aviva feels his eyes on her ass and legs as she places her things on a lounge chair. She's glad she didn't put on a bathing cap. Marshall is white and flabby and unhappy in his red trunks. He sits at the side paddling his feet in the water, and pronounces it cold. Aviva bends down to test with her hand—he's right. Their father retreats to a chair at the back to read some radiology reports.

Aviva stands at the deep end and pretends to be Seung, imagines the way he positions himself in a crouch and then plunges into the water without hesitation. She is aware too of the lifeguard's interest and wants to look confident. She dives. The cold clamps around her, knocks her forgetful for a moment. She kicks to the surface, startled, having briefly lost her sense of direction. For a moment panic flits through her as she instinctively feels what it would be like to turn and turn under the water and never find *up* again. It's okay, she thinks. I'm here—*above*. Very quickly her body warms, and she swims the way Seung taught her, each arm wheeling up straight and strong, each kick tight and clean. She is surprised at how quickly the wall comes forward to meet her, how fast she moves. How strong she is. She counts sixty laps and then hoists herself to the deck, tingling, content.

Marshall is still dithering at the shallow end. "I'll pull you in," she warns him.

"No!" He shrinks back, genuinely horrified. She is sorry. You can't spread happiness, can't force someone into your pleasures.

She looks around the atrium. "Where did Dad go?"

"Back to the apartment to do some work. He said see you for dinner."

Her hair is weightless; she roughs it up with her towel a few times and it's nearly dry. As she tosses the towel into the hamper by the door the lifeguard trots up to her and says, "Hey." He smiles and hands her a piece of paper. In the changing room she opens it. He's written down his name, his phone number. She folds the paper and slides it into her jeans. For the rest of her Chicago stay she carries it around and looks at it, thinking about his desire for her, imagining the solidity of him, how he might come inside of her and put an end to the awful spell that keeps her lacking, but she knows she won't call him. No one thinks she's a good girl, but she's more loyal, more chained, than anyone knows.

47

When I saw her shorn like that it struck me for the first time that things weren't exactly as we had all believed. To see them walking around campus, Seung's hand shoved in the back pocket of her jeans, to see them in the common room, him stretched out like some sort of pasha, Aviva perched on his hips—they were fully dressed but might as well have been naked—you thought that here were two people completely abandoned to each other, oblivious to anything else. We wanted that, too. We wanted to be drugged by sex; we wanted to be shameless, impolite, entitled. We wanted to worship and be worshipped. How they got away with it, we didn't know. Why they didn't get caught, disciplined. In the butt rooms, over dinner, boys would say, "Fuck, who do they think they are?" They'd say, "If I tried that you know it would be the boot for me."

But the haircut. And she looked thin. Drawn. You don't hack off hair like that, hair that looks and smells like sex, for no reason. She held herself almost as though she were being punished. I imagine how Seung reacted the first time he saw the change. She wouldn't have told him in advance. She didn't call him on the phone the whole time she was in Chicago. That's what I imagine. He would have held his hand above her shoulder where the heavy fall of hair used to be, cupped the emptiness. That would be his way. He wouldn't say anything about it, and no expression would cross his face. He was good at that kind of self-containment; it was bred into him. He'd be the first to acknowledge that. He'd just hold that negative space, feel it, remember. He couldn't even bring himself to mind the loss. He loved her so much, he still thought she looked beautiful, even with that frizzed, lopsided bush, so awkward and strange.

48

Seung is preparing. Now that he's proven himself there's no reason he can't succeed with Aviva. One morning during the vacation he takes the train to the city and visits a particular market in Chinatown, where he buys a supplement promised to increase potency. He mixes the foul-tasting herb with a cup of green tea every morning. And he refrains from masturbating. Whatever will give him a little advantage. His erections torment him at night, hard and unsubsiding. Sterne says he calls out in his sleep.

"What did I say?"

"You talked about the high dive. You said, 'the competition.' 'I'll break my back,' you said."

Sterne looks away in the morning when Seung dresses, pretending not to notice. Seung keeps well under the table in class, wears long sweaters under his blazer even though the weather has grown warm. He begins to be confident that he will possess Aviva soon. After that, the other times will be like false starts at a race; now the whistle will blow and he will blaze out from the wall and claim his victory.

During the second week of May, Aviva's roommate has to go home to Maine for her grandmother's funeral. And Seung and Aviva decide that he will come to her room. They've never done this before. It's more dangerous—Hiram faces two other dorms where students come frequently in and out, and Aviva's not sure that Carlyle and Lena will make sentries as good as Sterne and Giddings. But perhaps a change of place will be what they need. His room is full of their failures.

The day is pleasant and mild, the dormitories hold a leftover chill. After the year's traffic the linoleum floors are scuffed, the stairwell walls smudged with handprints and pen marks. Aviva waits in her room, uneasy. Her room is smaller and older than Seung's, shabbier. The one window leaks a wan light over her roommate's bed. Aviva has never done anything to decorate her own side of the room. Her roommate has a corkboard tacked with snapshots of her friends: on a beach, on skis, making faces. Aviva's wall is bare. She has one framed photo of her parents and brother on top of her dresser, taken when they went to the Dominican Republic the winter before last. Marshall is propping up the tail of a gigantic iguana. Their father is warily holding the head. Aviva, between them, supports the belly. She remembers that it felt smooth and hard and cool. Their mother stands to the side, gazing at the group rather than at the camera, as if she is analyzing the scene for an upcoming lecture. A barefoot man on the beach had come up to them with the iguana, offering to take their picture with it for twenty pesos.

Seung slides into the room silently, nodding his reassurance: *No problem*. The door clicks quietly behind him. He is bursting, afraid he will not be able to wait, afraid he will touch her too roughly. When they kiss he counts the seconds to steady himself. He is like a monk meditating under torture, following his breath to keep his mind clear and sovereign. He rolls Aviva onto her back and kisses her neck and belly. She turns her face away, trying not to think. He puts his mouth between her legs. He's done this a couple of times before, but she always stops him after a while: it's hurting, she'll say. She's wondered if something is wrong with her, that she can't come this way, only with herself, with her hands or her thoughts. She tugs a little at his hair, to signal that she wants him to come back up, but he ignores her.

"Show me what you do," he says.

"Show you .. ?"

"Just do what you do."

She reaches down and brushes two fingers across the mound. He expected something more intricate and forceful. She might be stroking a kitten. She makes the same movement over and over, never deviating or altering the pressure. It could make one sleepy, watching the unwavering rhythm of it. Gradually he perceives a stirring, something buried nosing its way up; her mouth parts. He takes her hand and places it gently at her side, bends and replicates with his tongue the slow restrained motions her fingers made. Her head turns slowly from side to side, like someone's refusal filmed in slow motion. Her belly grows hard, her legs tense. Her moans contain a growl, a register he's never heard before. It thrills him. At the peak she seizes his head, thrusting into him, his parched and aching lips. He clutches the sides of the bed to stay against her.

Afterward she will not let him go. She clamps his legs in hers, presses her chest to his chest. Grasps his head tight. Her short, coarse hair is in his mouth. "Hold me, hold me," she begs, over and over. He can still feel the throbbing of her cunt against his lips. She begins to weep. "I didn't think that could happen," she says. Gradually her grip relaxes. She nestles back on the bed. Her eyes, dilated, blink at him. He watches the lashes go up and down.

"You are beautiful," he says.

Her eyes close. She dozes. Protectively he watches the parted legs, the breasts settled down against her rib cage. He strokes himself a little, paying homage.

Aviva opens her eyes in alarm.

"How long .. ?"

"A minute, two minutes."

With some effort, Aviva sits up, and stares pointedly at Seung's lap. Carefully she fits her hand around his cock. She's never quite gotten used to doing this, it never feels as natural as everything else. In the beginning she expected

that her hand would move as if over ice, an unimpeded glid-
ing, but discovered that skin had more friction than that.
Her palm snagged and frustrated her attempt at a rhythm.
It didn't do much for Seung, either, and she hated feeling
clumsy, not knowing how to make the pleasure happen. So
mostly she avoids touching him there. But now she has an
idea. She reaches for the hand lotion on her dresser and puts
a dollop in her palm. She holds her palm out to Seung.

"Do you think . . ?"

Seung nods. She strokes him up and down slowly, then
faster. "God," Seung murmurs. "God." For once his eyes close.
The power Aviva feels sends a shock through her entire system. She wants this, she wants him. Guided by instinct she
reaches with her free hand to cup his balls. All of Seung's patience flees; the starved animal rises up. Trembling, willing
himself not to lose control, he pushes her back on the bed and
kneels above her. Her hands rise up and flutter down—should
she help him? Not help him? She watches his bent, frowning head. She has the sudden image of his penis as a swollen
weapon, a black and purple nightstick, a punishment, something large enough to damage her. Her heart pounds.

But he wilts at the entrance. She reaches down to hold
him, to force matters, feels how sopping she is. He grows,
subsides, grows, diminishes. And diminishes more. A radio suddenly goes on outside, spilling a bass beat into the
morning. It's over, she thinks.

He kneels at the side of the bed, his face buried in the
sheets, and cries silently. His whole body shakes. It goes on

forever. It's unbearable. She wants to strike him. She wants him disappeared, out of her room, removed from her: all his tears, needs, the dumb, weak slab of him. Her rage freezes her over. She does not hold him.

He rises, puts on his shirt, his jeans. His clothes are damp and his hands are like paddles. He stands like a man lost in a cavernous train station, a stranger in town. She will not look at him.

"Aviva."

She will not look at him. She has stopped being a girl and she cannot be a woman; she has no fate; she's been emptied out.

"Aviva. Aviva. Sweetheart."

No answer.

49

At the Disciplinary Committee hearing, Señora Ivarra reports that at about three thirty on that Sunday afternoon she encountered Seung Jung descending the side stairs leading from the second floor to the ground floor of Hiram, heading toward the side exit. She asked the boy what the devil ("my exact phrase," the señora testifies) he was doing there. "Leaving, ma'am," Seung told her. Señora Ivarra did not appreciate the humor. She asked Seung how long he had been in the dormitory.

"A few minutes."

"And what exactly, if I must repeat myself, were you doing?"

"I was planning to go to Aviva Rossner's room. I was going to surprise her. Then I thought better of it."

"Oh, why was that?"

"I realized it was a stupid idea. I realized I could get caught and that it would get Aviva in trouble."

"Come with me, please."

They knocked on Aviva's door. Number 21.

"It's Señora Ivarra. I will need to come in."

Aviva opened the door. Dorota was sitting on her bed. There were cards dealt out for gin rummy. The bed was made, the quilt drawn up.

"Hi, Señora Ivarra."

Seung had had the presence of mind to fall behind the señora and as he caught Aviva's eyes he shook his head very slightly from side to side. *Say no.*

No, she said to everything the señora asked. No, no, no.

50

Not long ago, at a theater fundraiser, a man came up to me and greeted me, and I recognized an old Auburn classmate—a lacrosse player, he reminded me—a kid I'd probably never talked to in my entire time at the school. Nevertheless we got to talking now, and it came up that he'd been on what we called Stud Jud, or the student judiciary committee. These were the kids—good students, high moral fiber—who sat in on expulsion and probationary hearings. They didn't get to vote on the outcome, but they had advisory privileges. I asked him what had happened at Seung Jung's hearing.

He paused, frowned. Naturally he remembered. The proceedings were confidential, he explained. Stud Jud was never supposed to reveal what went on.

It was a good while ago, I argued. And whom could the information hurt now?

"Those two," he said. "If only they'd just bothered to hide it a little more. You know? I think that's what drove everyone crazy, that they wouldn't hide it."

I pressed him—he wasn't giving me my answer.

The ex-lacrosse player finally relented, and even seemed relieved to speak. At a certain point, he said, it seemed as if Seung had some chance of being let off, that he might only get probation. Two teachers attested to his solid academic standing, his consistent class attendance, the fact that he turned his work in on time. Mr. Glass described the positive atmosphere Seung had encouraged in Weld among the younger classes, his ready ear for kids in need. Seung had no history of probation for any reason, he told the panel, and only one incident of restrictions, back in the fall, for his behavior with Aviva Rossner at the school dance. When Mr. Glass was asked if he had any reason to believe that Seung had previously violated school rules with Aviva Rossner, Mr. Glass answered that Seung was not up for any infraction of the rules other than this one. Then a silence fell and the faculty members looked down at their notes or off into the distance, and, according to the ex-lacrosse player, everyone knew what everyone was thinking, which was that Aviva Rossner and Seung Jung had been flouting the rules for months, had been violating Auburn's ethic of healthy moderation by spilling sex into every cranny of the school, and that, to maintain the proper separation between adult and child, decency and decadence, somehow it had to come to a stop.

Dean Ruwart spoke first. He brought everyone's attention to the fact that Seung was a proctor. He read from the *Auburn Rule Book*: "The proctor is a model for his peers and is held to the highest level of accountability."

That must have been the reason they were especially hard on Seung.

51

Dorota said, "Thank God I was coming out of the bathroom just then and saw them, Seung and the señora. I saved your skin."

"You did," said Aviva. She wished it had been Carlyle or Lena. With Dorota there was always a mysterious debt of some sort, some leftover sense of obligation. But perhaps only Dorota would have thought so quickly, would have walked directly and without obvious hurry to Aviva's room and told her they must make the bed, right now, and open the window to air the place out, and do you have a pack of cards or a crossword puzzle? Everybody on the floor knew about the questioning within minutes. A community such as this one instantly picks up the vibration of inquisition. Carlyle and Lena said: You were supposed to come tell us when Seung was ready to leave! We were supposed to be the lookouts. What in the world happened? Were you crazy?

The *Auburn Rule Book* states that being called up for an offense punishable by expulsion is stressful and difficult for a student and his or her family, as well as for the larger school community, and so every attempt is made to ensure that hearings will be held quickly. The Disciplinary Committee is made up of six faculty members and four non-voting students who rotate on an annual basis. The process is this: the faculty member bringing the charge must report the violation to the student's advisor, and the student's parents will be notified. After obtaining a written statement from the student, the advisor will submit it to the Disciplinary Committee, which will also receive a written statement from the accusing faculty member. The dean of students reviews the statements and presents the case to the committee. The accusing faculty member, the student, the student's advisor, the dean, and two of the student's teachers must appear at the disciplinary hearing. The student may make an oral statement at that time, or his teachers may speak on his behalf. After all of the documents and statements have been offered to the committee, the student is asked to leave the room and the committee decides whether or not the student has committed the offense of which he is accused. If the answer is yes, the first motion must be for Requirement to Withdraw. If that fails, the next motion will be for probation. If a student is required to withdraw he must leave the campus within thirty-six hours.

Seung's advisor is Mr. Leonov, a man he has never trusted to give him any advice at all, although in this case the older man has some that is wise. Aviva and Seung, he suggests, should probably not spend too much time together in the coming days. He asks if Seung would like to contact his parents, before he, Mr. Leonov, makes the required phone call. Seung laughs. "You've got to be kidding," he says. He's not being disrespectful, and Mr. Leonov seems to understand. If you're a Korean kid, you keep your head down and don't look for extra trouble. *Umma* and *Apah* will come after you soon enough.

The call comes in the afternoon. Some prep on the fourth floor beckons him to the pay phone. Seung imagines his mother's shrieks are audible throughout the entire building: The lack of gratitude. Their sacrifices. The embarrassment for the whole family. The shame.

"Yes, *Omoni*," he murmurs.

"And over a white girl, a—" Seung doesn't catch the Korean word, but it's clear it means *loose* or worse.

Seung's father gets on. "You will amount to nothing," he says. "Colgate will not take you now. What will you do with your life?"

Seung tries to explain that it's not a sure thing that he'll be expelled. There's a real chance that he'll get probation. And if the worst occurs, he'll do his senior year over at home, and apply again to Colgate for next year.

"How do you think that will happen?" asks his father. "Do you think you will just come back and live at home? You have no home."

It will be all right. Seung has to let them storm and curse him like this; later they will calm down, they will come around. It's always been so, although never before has his infraction been so great. What a good job he has done until now in hiding his delinquencies from them. They will not refuse to let him be their son again. They will not kick him out of house and home. He can almost convince himself of this.

52

Now Aviva walks past Weld each day without stopping, gripping her knapsack to her shoulder, reduced, alone, and once more the Auburn storytellers spin their tales. Aviva is a tragic figure, threatened with separation from her great love. Or she is a careless, self-involved bitch who has brought Seung to ruin. She is suicidal; she is indifferent. No disciplinary charges were ever brought against Aviva; no one could prove that things were not as Seung said: that he impulsively went up to surprise her, that he had never been in her room. He too walks alone now to and from his meals and classes, looking like a man made of separate parts that do not hang together, like a body that has died and is activated by something external.

In Weld there are passionate huddled conversations. Students rail at the unfairness of the authorities; someone calls for starting some sort of petition. We are all swept up in these feelings of outrage, from the preps and lowers who know Seung only as a superhero, an embodiment of elder glamour, to seniors like Cort and Voss and me, who have never been part of Seung's group but are newly seen as authorities on the mysteries of Auburn's disciplinary procedures. None of us can remember having heard of a time when a kid caught in a boyfriend's or girlfriend's room did not get a Requirement to Withdraw.

One or another of us periodically denies the outcome we all foresee. "He gets good grades. Teachers like him. He's brought honor to the school with his sportsmanship and athletic performance. He wasn't in her room, just in the stairwell."

I'm playing Frisbee in front of Weld with David Yee, which is a shame, because he hobbles my game. Normally I'll play only with Cort or Voss or Giddings, who will sometimes join in, or Dennis MacBride from Eustis dorm, who's even better than I am. But Cort and Voss and I—well, we don't have much to do with each other since that afternoon I walked into their room. And sometimes I have got to feel that spinning disk in my hand, feel it fly free of me and arrow into some strict, chosen space, and I jump at the chance to play with the basest klutz if I have to.

Yee makes a decent catch of a low-skimming throw, a line-drive-ish sort of release, and then throws it back wild, so that it bounces down the little grassy slope on the north side of Weld. I turn, waggling my arms above my head to indicate to David that his incompetence has been noted and scorned,

and when I'm on my way back, the Frisbee retrieved, I see
Aviva and Seung sitting on the Weld bench. Just all of a sudden there. They sit like two old people, half a foot between
them, completely silent. I shoot the Frisbee back to Yee, trying to make my mark while getting a sense of what's going
on. After a few moments I feel Aviva's eyes on me. A heat
comes up in my back and arms, which loosen and stretch
and deepen their grace. I feel her eyes on my chest; I feel
them bold and rebellious as she sits next to Seung. I know I
could be imagining it, but I don't think so. You can feel that
kind of attention on you; you know when it's insistent, when
it doesn't move. I'm so warm I feel a little woozy. And then—
I see it from the corner of my eye—Seung gets up and goes
inside. It's like a scene in a play for which I've been the un-
derstudy; for weeks and months I've been readying myself
for my part, and here it is. Aviva is alone.

The way she dresses has changed in the months she's
been at school. The plunging angora sweaters don't show up
anymore, nor the cowboy boots. The look has been tamed.
But she still likes her makeup, and there is still a deliberate-
ness about her style that makes her stand out from Auburn's
sloppy-baggy or preppy norm. She still wears the three gold
chains and the gold hoop earrings, and when I get closer I'll
see that there's an addition now: a gold ring with ruby chips,
worn on her fourth finger, the wedding one. She's got on a
pair of khaki-colored shorts and a boatneck top.

Since Seung was caught in her dorm my imaginary inter-
ludes with Aviva have become more leisurely. It's as if, his

status at school shaky, Seung no longer owns her so exclusively anymore. I've always been aware of the small details of Aviva's physical presence: the slightly freckled forearms, the barely pointed chin, the particular splay of her fingers. But now, in my private theater, I hold on to those details longer. I slip her blouse off her shoulders and she doesn't fade. I unbutton her from the neck to the belly and lay bare that purple bra again. I arrange her on my bed and sketch with my eyes her surprisingly ample hips. She reaches up for me and lets me come in. Her half-lidded eyes and the soft parting of her mouth reveal a pleasure I've never seen on the face of Lisa Flood. Sometimes Aviva doesn't vanish even as I get more urgent and less kind.

I've told myself that if Seung is forced to leave Auburn, I might even have a real-world chance with Aviva. I don't really believe this, but the notion allows the moments after I come to be filled with something that is nearly satisfaction rather than, as usual, a vague resentment and unease.

I aim the Frisbee at a spot past the library so David will have to go far to fetch it. "Sorry!" I call to him, shrugging, feigning puzzlement at my lousy aim. Then I walk toward the bench. I don't know how I walk. I might look false and awkward; I might glide like Fred Fucking Astaire for all I know. I don't remember. But then I'm there, looking down at her. She's already got a book open and is seemingly absorbed in it. Leave Aviva alone for ninety seconds and she opens a book. Could I have been right that she was watching me so intently before? I believe I was right.

"What are you reading?" I ask. A very imaginative open-er. Not to mention that I can read the book's title perfectly clearly: *Jane Eyre*.

She raises the cover higher for me. "It's so-so," she says. "Lena's always trying to get me to read the Brontës. Am I supposed to find Rochester sympathetic? He's a jerk. The one I hate most is *Wuthering Heights*. It's an embarrassment to anyone female."

"No, tell me what you really think of it," I say. "Don't hold back."

I get it out of her—a little smile. Thin, transient, but there.

I take that moment to sit down next to her, remaining alert to any rejectionist vibe. We've never spoken since that day at the boathouse. I don't feel anything overtly hostile coming from her. Perhaps, after all, I didn't shake her enough that day to make her hate me. Perhaps it already seems like a long time ago to her, as it does, somewhat, to me. She seems a little chilly, that's all, sitting there holding her book impatiently, as if wondering how many seconds of politeness are required until she can go back to it.

"How's your brother?" I ask. "The one who writes you all the time?"

She smiles more fulsomely now. It wasn't what she expect-ed to hear next, I guess. She tells me that Marshall is good, he's going to summer school because he failed seventh-grade English and social studies, but he's cheerful enough about it, and he knows the material . . . He mailed her a build-it-yourself radio kit for her birthday, and it made her burst out

in laughter: When did he think she was going to find time
to build it? And when had she ever shown any interest in
electronics? But it kills her, really; he probably spent hours
choosing it. Aviva sighs. Marshall. He shaved off all his hair
over Christmas vacation, but it's growing back.

I can't imagine why she's giving me so much detail. Maybe she just likes talking about her brother. Maybe all anyone
wants to talk to her about these days is Seung, and she's tired
of that. She seems to lighten when she talks of her brother,
lose her wariness. In my peripheral vision I sense David approaching, damn Frisbee in hand, fed up with waiting for
me. It looks like he's going to be stupid enough to ask what's
up, is the game still on. But he stops at a distance, watching
us for a moment, then turns toward the library. Good man,
David. Just so long as you give me back that Frisbee. It's my
best one, a Discraft Sky-Styler.

"How'd he look?" I ask Aviva, about her brother's shearing.

"Terrible."

"So why'd you do it, too?"

Her eyes widen. A moment passes, and I think she realizes I don't mean it unkindly, that I'm actually pained by
it, missing those heavy tresses. *Tresses*: a good, romantic,
old-fashioned word.

"I don't know," she says. "It seemed to make sense at the
time."

"I wish you hadn't."

"I went home," she says slowly, as if she really wants me to
see the matter through her eyes, "and everything in my house

seemed dingy and wrong, just out of place and worn out and
. . . and spoiled. I can't explain it." She tells me that her parents
split up back in the fall; her father closed her mother's credit
card and checking accounts and is already behind on his child
support payments. He's living with another woman, who
makes strange comments about Jews. Aviva is worried he's
not going to come through with her Auburn tuition for next
year. He claims that he will, no problem, but the letters arriving in Chicago from Auburn's bursar's office prove he hasn't.

"Anya says not to worry, she'll keep me here somehow.
She says his new lady is old money, new vulgar. In that accent of hers."

"Who's Anya?"

"My mother. I call her Mom or *Matka*—that's Czech—to
her face, but when my brother and I talk about her behind
her back we call her Anya. Because she's just such an Anya."
She explains that her mother was born near Prague and got
sent out of the country when she was nine, on one of the
Kindertransports set up to rescue children from the Nazis.
When the war was over, her parents, Aviva's grandparents,
were dead. Anya's not as young as most mothers. She was
thirty-four when Aviva was born. She teaches sociology at
a college in the Chicago suburbs—"about images of women
and women's roles in society and that sort of thing." As if all
this explains something to me.

"You come from the same town as Seung, don't you?"

"Yeah," I say. I wish Seung didn't need to come back into
the conversation.

"Do you know his family?"

I know who they are, I say. They live in a different part
of town. I don't say it's where the smaller houses are, where
you have more immigrants and blacks and even some
crime. I mention that they're not the kind of parents you
saw all the time at school basketball games or the damn
used-book fundraiser.

"His mother told him she wished for something very bad
to happen to me."

This startles me. "She said that?"

"Apparently. But in Korean. With some choice epithets. I
think one of them meant 'pale chicken.'"

I can't help laughing. She laughs too, then it vanishes.

"Do you think Seung is going to be kicked out?" she asks.
"Everybody tells me no, and I'm tired of being lied to. What
are the odds, do you think?"

"When a kid goes before the committee?" I rub my hand
on the iron arm of the bench. "Usually they get kicked out."

She nods. She faces straight ahead, so that I see her in
profile.

"What would you say if I told you I might be glad if
Seung got kicked out?"

I take my time in responding. First, there's a sharp
thrill—is she hinting something to me? Something connected to the way she watched me while I played? Then I
decide I'm out of my mind. She couldn't be coming on to
me. Probably what's driving her is something less sneaky
and more desperate—she simply needs to talk. Because I

happen to be here. Because I'm listening. And somehow she knows it won't go any further.

Slowly, I answer, "I wouldn't say anything. Or I'd say you have your reasons."

"Well, don't worry," she says, dropping her gaze to her knees. "I was just joking." A pause. "I feel like I can tell you things. I don't know why." Then: "It's probably a terrible idea."

As though that were a cue, a window opens above us. It's Sterne, his T-shirt sleeves rolled up over his ropy shoulders. "Hey, Bennett-Jones, take a hike," he calls down.

Aviva's head snaps up. "Tell Seung to chill out," she shouts back to Sterne.

"I'm sorry," I murmur, wishing she'd let me speak up for myself.

"Don't be. He's being ridiculous."

"Are you moving your flabby ass or what?" asks Sterne. "You're bothering the lady."

"Jesus," says Aviva. She turns away from the window and yanks open her book. She looks tired and a little cowed, and I don't want to cause any more trouble for her. It's time for me to go. I swallow the sting of once again being silenced by Sterne. I feel that if I give it back to him the way he deserves, I'll lose Aviva's respect. So I'll take the high road and all that. Look like the better man. Fuck. I get a sudden craving for something sweet. I think I'll head into town.

"Take care," I say to Aviva—a phrase that until now I've heard only from a grown-up's mouth. I touch her arm.

Sterne fades and all I'm aware of is that I've sat here for ten or fifteen minutes, talking to her, hearing what she had to say. My head is light; I'm beginning to fly. I don't care if Aviva dislikes me, or is using me. Maybe she is, maybe she isn't. I don't think she knows herself. Anyway, it doesn't matter. She's telling me things. She's telling me things even Seung doesn't know.

53

Those last weeks of school the sun doesn't set until eight, eight fifteen in the evening. You can walk late in the woods or along the river. The smell of lilac and wisteria follows one to classes. The town is in bloom: baskets of impatiens on the porches, azaleas in the yards. Until the very last minute, it's hard to take our final tests and papers seriously. We're seniors. We have our spots in our colleges, our summer plans. We are just waiting to be gone. For the next part of our lives to begin.

David Yee closes our door and gestures me over to his bureau. He opens his underwear drawer and fishes out a flat, tear-shaped bottle of Courvoisier XO. I whistle.

"We worked really hard all year," he says.

"You devil dog."

He smiles, nervous, pleased with himself.

"You little charlatan. You pretend good boy."

He holds on to his flickering smile.

It's really good stuff that he has, aged thirty years or something like that. I don't ask where he's gotten it. It is the kind of booze your parents might give you when they've decided it's time to treat you like a man. I look forward to drinking it. We make a plan to meet at a spot along the creek and walk somewhere we won't be seen. David is so anxious about the whole thing, this first foray into delinquency, that he insists we go there separately rather than together. Fine, I say. I tell him I'll bring what I have—the usual, 151. We'll be aristocratic and ceremonial with the cognac and make sure we get plastered with the 151. As a goof I put on the hideous class ring my father ordered for me at the start of school, saying that once I graduated (he reserved his certainty in regard to this outcome), he would have it engraved with my initials and the year.

It's two weeks until the end of the term. Seung's bags are packed. His trunk is at the dock behind the gym and will be sent by freight to his home. He'll be in Jordan by tomorrow afternoon. His brother is coming down from Ithaca and will meet him at Jordan Station. "To be a buffer against the duffers, man," he says. Number One Son. He's not so bad.

Sterne and Giddings take Seung out for a farewell dinner. They go to the Chinese place on the state road, a forty-five-minute walk, and Seung doesn't let anyone order alcohol. "Do me a favor," he says. He wants them in the library, he says, by six thirty. They had better do well on their final

exams; there have been enough fuckups already. The restaurant has paper lanterns and a plastic Santa Claus atop
a bricked-up fireplace. The paper menus are stained with
food. The boys toast the absent Detweiler with raised glasses of Orange Crush.

"May he return."

"May he not return. May he have a better fate."

"May he regain his sanity. May he be valedictorian of his
two-bit high school and hike the Lake Superior Trail and
sleep with many plump Midwestern babes."

They're drunk. Even though it's only Orange Crush
they're drinking, they are woozy, sentimental, uncoordinated. Seung makes them both promise to look after Aviva.
Make sure she's all right, that she doesn't need for anything.
Giddings sweeps his arm to make a point and a glass goes
spinning off the table. The waitress kneels to gather up the
shards, telling them it's no problem, no problem.

Out on the strip again, Giddings gives Seung his go-
ing-away present: two tabs of excellent acid he's been saving since his last trip home. "One for you, one for Aviva."
There's more where that came from. Giddings had planned
a graduation gift for them all.

"Without you it won't be much of a celebration," Sterne
comments.

"Sure it will," Seung tells him. "You guys have made it.
You got through."

They clutch him to themselves, clap him on the back.
Next year they'll be in college; he'll be in high school again.

Seung returns alone to the dormitory after the others peel off for the library. His feet hurt. Aviva said she'd meet him in front of Hiram at six thirty. They'll go for a walk or sit in the common room. No one cares anymore what they do. No one watches. The campus is busy, students bent over their books for finals. Interest in the two of them is waning. Their story is wrapped up, it's over. They were caught, they didn't get away with it after all. Their mystery has been leached out of them.

Aviva holds a large book against her chest. Seung can't see what it is; her arms are crossed in front. Without exchanging any words, they begin to walk. They pass the edge of campus and walk along a residential street. There's a child swinging in the mellow evening light. When they are a few blocks from campus Aviva leans against a lamppost. She's still holding the book to her chest.

"Seung, once you're home . . ."

He waits. He knows. He is going to be subjected to her truth, those things she cannot refrain from saying because they happen to be so.

"It's destroying me . . ." he hears. "The humiliation . . . lying there . . . I'm dead inside . . . you've made me dead . . . I can't feel anything anymore . . ." There are no tears, not even a look of sadness. Her mouth is a hard, grim thing.

It *is* the truth. He can see that. He is destroying her. She's lost weight; she has become all elbows and neck. Her cropped and brushy hair is growing out again, badly. She is slumped and drawn, like someone recovering from the flu. He's murdered her beauty. No, it isn't that. That is still there. What, then? Her vitality. Her pride. Her love, if that ever existed.

"I don't want you to call me. I don't want you to write me . . ."

His hands ball into fists; he grits his teeth. Sweat springs out on his temples. He's shaking, and then he begins to cry. Aviva thinks that it is crying, anyway. There are tears on Seung's cheeks but he makes no sounds other than a choked sort of growling. His lips are closed, tight.

"Y-y-ou . . ." he finally forces out. "Y-y-you . . ."

She doesn't know if he is cursing her or begging her. Perhaps he is going to strike her. If he does, she'll hit him back. He begins to gasp and pound his head with his fist. Something shifts in Aviva and she feels that his actions have crossed the line into theater; he is trying to shame her into fear and pity.

"Oh, Christ, Seung, I won't let you . . . you're not going to *do* this . . ." She runs from him, back through the streets, all the way to her dormitory. She checks in with Señora Ivarra, drops her heavy book on the floor and gets in bed, clothed, curled up tight. As she ran she imagined him behind her, chasing her; there had been violence in his eyes.

Seung lowers himself onto someone's front steps and sits for a long time until his breathing loosens and slows. He always knew this day would come, knew he would lose her, that he wasn't born to possess the things he wants. Not a creature like him, a Korean boy, a Number Two Son. Life put this girl in his way so he could envision pleasure, taste it, and watch it run away.

When he feels capable of it, he makes his way back to Weld, jittery and spent, and knocks on Mr. Glass's door.

"I'm in for the night," he tells the teacher.

Mr. Glass looks at the boy's raw eyes and damp skin. The dorm is almost empty. It's Seung's last night at Auburn.

"Seung. Would you like to come in?"

"No, thank you."

"I didn't want this outcome," Mr. Glass tells him, not shutting the door, not letting him leave yet. The boy wears that mask the Asian kids often do, the one that says, "I will not speak. Do not ask." But that unhealthiness about the skin and eyes betrays him. What a waste, Mr. Glass thinks. A talented kid, but one who liked to push his luck, always sure the cat had more lives. Still, so close to graduation, the committee could have bent for once, could have given him probation. But the old-timers wouldn't have it. The Auburn disciplinary system is out of date, inflexible, in need of re-form. Mr. Glass has always taken that position.

"I know," says Seung.

"Are you sure you don't want to come in?" Mr. Glass asks. "Ellen bought some new tea, blackberry something."

"Thanks, Mr. Glass. I'm just going to lie down."

As soon as he does, the shaking overtakes Seung so fiercely that he thinks his ribs will crack. The pain deep in his bones makes him want to howl. Frightened, he forces himself to get up and walk back and forth across the room.

Maybe it will be better if he stays in motion. When he passes the bureau mirror he sees himself as an elongated streak of darkness taking shape for a moment then sliding away. He stops and looks more intently. He's motionless now, but he still can't see himself. Is it because he is trembling so hard, or is something really wrong with his face? He drops his gaze and names the objects on the dresser: his sketchbook and two charcoal pencils, his penknife, a novel by Thomas Bernhard that he is leaving for Sterne. His heart beats very rapidly; he is sweating profusely again. Suddenly he fears that if he stays in this room he will die. He will literally die.

He hardly sees the stairs in his panic to get outside. It doesn't even occur to him to stop and tell Mr. Glass he is going. He plunges past the dorms, the gymnasium, the practice fields and the track, into the woods in the late-slanting light, looking for a place to hide himself. He veers off the running path and into a thicket of brambly vines where he eventually finds a small clearing. He lies on his back on the cool ground and gives himself over to the disturbance inside. His legs jerk so hard that the joints pop. His head is full of loose stones. He is deaf to anything but the sound of his graceless, thrashing body. Something rattles at the back of his throat.

When the fit finally passes, he dozes: ten minutes, fifteen. He wakes, fishes in his pocket for a joint, and smokes it rapidly, waiting for the cloud of ease to come up and comfort him. The flame moves closer and closer to his fingers and he lets it burn there, licking and then enveloping the skin.

Finally he drops the last scrap into the dirt, where it flares up with a small bright light and shrivels out. He stabs his burnt fingertips into the earth. He aches all over. He pictures Aviva in bed at his parents' house, her legs parted, the pale tender skin there and the dark hair, and hears the extraordinary sounds that, later, he discovered how to coax from her body.

He walks. After a few minutes he hears voices nearby, footsteps, and moves away from them. Instinct takes him in the direction of the Bog. He suspects it will be empty tonight, the night before the first day of finals. It's so peaceful there; he's always loved it, especially at this time of year, with the wildflowers and the light lingering late in the trees. He winds his way in and when he gets to the Bog he finds to his satisfaction that it is, in fact, deserted. He could be Robinson Crusoe on his own desert island; he could be a lone explorer on a kind and fertile moon. He lowers himself to his haunches and dips his smarting fingers into the shallow water. The water is very cold, and, after a moment of numbing, the pain returns even more fiercely. Seung can feel the blisters forming.

And that is where I discover him, squatting by the water, trailing his fingers in it. I've been following the path to my meeting with David, and, pushing through some tangled brush in an attempt to take a shortcut, I find myself in a magnificent clearing. I've never actually been here before. The Bog is not technically a bog but rather a little lake with some algae buildup along the shallow margin. It lies in a hollow, the birch trees rising up all around it to create a secluded and otherworldly effect. You can pass within a few feet of it in the woods and not see it or even hear the kids hanging out there. Or so I've been told. For obvious reasons the earnest druggies at Auburn, the career visionaries, the ones who need several hours on a Sunday to take an uninterrupted acid or mushroom trip, favor it, and they have passed along certain proprietary methods for finding one's way here. On a few occasions, Voss and Cort and I tried, for sport's sake, to locate it, but always failed. Now here I am, having meant to go somewhere else, and I have Seung for company. It is rare to see him alone, without that gang of his. I am surprised they are not with him, on this last night. He looks less himself without them, smaller.

I can't tell if Seung senses my presence. I could just dip back into the woods, try another route to my destination, but instead I head toward him. I make noise as I approach, coughing, but he doesn't look around.

"Rough luck," I say, when I reach him. "Administration bastards."

He nods slightly, without lifting his head.

I toss my knapsack on the ground and crouch next to it.

"You all right?" I ask.

"Sure," he says. Finally he looks at me. I see the telltale redness in his eyes, but his pupils are enlarged rather than constricted. What's he been taking?

I don't say anything, Seung doesn't say anything. He doesn't ask me why I'm here. The silence goes on for a long time. It's only for the first few minutes that it feels strange, that I fidget and am tempted several times to make a noise, any noise. Then, slowly, that urge dissipates and begins to be replaced with the most remarkable sense of ease. I watch the spots of light on the surface of the water and hear, once or twice, a bullfrog. There's a faint buzzing that is the sound either of tiny insects or of the silence itself. Seung squats next to me, quietly, occasionally shifting his weight. It's as if we are friends who have known each other so long we no longer need to speak in each other's presence. Perhaps I remember this silence as longer than it was. It felt beautifully endless. I've completely forgotten about David Yee and our rendezvous. And sitting here, next to Seung, I begin to sense what's going on in his mind. No words come to me, but I feel his heaviness, his confusion and his fear. I can feel the way he's pinned, that even his breath comes at a price. For him to raise his head, lift an arm to throw a pebble into the water: these things require supreme effort.

At long last, I open my knapsack for the flask of 151, take a swig, and offer it to Seung. He accepts it, unsmiling, and takes a modest tipple. I urge him to continue, tell him there is plenty. That's what we do for the next little while, pass the flask back and forth. My throat and belly sting and warm. By this time I've remembered David Yee but I figure the hell with him, he can wait.

The sun slips steadily down the sky, as if making up for dawdling during the day. The rum has made me thirsty. I take off my shoes and socks, walk a couple of feet into the water to where it grows clear, and scoop handfuls into my mouth. By this time, I need a piss, so I walk a distance away and take care of that. When I return Seung is in the water. He hasn't bothered to roll up his wrinkled army surplus pants or anything. He gets well in, up to his waist or so, then tosses himself onto his back. I stand at the edge watching him. His black hair is plastered against the sides of his face; with those sharp cheekbones he looks Indian. He strokes his way to the center of the Bog and then butterflies back, his powerful arms churning up waves. Near the bank he sinks into a back float, his eyes closed. He is smiling, serene. Water is, after all, his element.

Afterward he stretches out on the bank.

"Seung," I say. "You're lying in the dirt, man." Why that bothers me I can't at the time rightly say. I will swear to you now that it was a protective instinct. I didn't want him to get his hair filthy. Anyway, Seung doesn't hear me, or pretends he doesn't. He lies as still as a sunbather in his soaking clothes in the growing dark and chill.

All right, I think. I stretch out next to him, using my knapsack for a pillow. More silence. I feel again that unexpected comfort, as if Seung and I often come here and lie quietly with our thoughts, not feeling any need to communicate.

At last, when the darkness is beginning to obscure his face, he rolls over onto one elbow. "Do you ever think about killing yourself, Bennett-Jones?" he asks.

"Ever?" I reply. "All the time."

"So why haven't you done it?"

I blink up into the gray sky. "Laziness."

"No. I want to know."

"I'm not putting you on." I sit up; it's easier to think this way. I'm a little logy from the booze. "I'm not a person with a lot of conviction. There have been times when dying seemed important, but never important enough."

Seung reaches for his dry sneakers and pulls out a joint he's stashed in one. "Care to?" he asks.

"Sure."

"I pegged you as a toker, Bennett-Jones."

"I thought I kept that a pretty good secret."

"I have superb radar. But you do it yourself, on your own. That's not good for you. It has to be a social thing. If you do it alone it turns you strange."

"Thanks for the concern."

Seung takes a deep drag and passes the joint to me. He closes his eyes when he draws in the smoke, then swallows gently, unhastily. It's almost feminine, this savoring.

I take a hissing inhale but warn myself to go slow. The booze is already making me heavy-headed, and I don't want to lose too much control.

"You'd kill yourself over getting the boot?" I ask.

"The boot?" he murmurs. He sits up now too.

"*Cannibis sativa*," he says in a deep voice, as if he's doing a voice-over for a television commercial. "First used in the third millennium BC by the ancient Hindus of India and Nepal. Known and appreciated also by the Assyrians, the

Scythians, the Thracians and the Dacians, the ancient Chinese, the ancient Greeks . . ."

"Yet heinously outlawed by a narrow-minded and ill-informed Congress in 1937 . . ."

"Hey! You know your facts, Bennett-Jones."

". . . which did not stop it from being used as a truth serum by the OSS during World War Two."

"Do you know how to diagram a THC molecule?"

"I'm sorry. That goes beyond my personal researches."

"It looks like a pull toy." Seung sketches it out in the air. "You've got the head with your three hexagon rings, and then your tail of five carbons . . . a pentyl group. Tetrahydrocannabinol."

"That I didn't know, but I can tell you that possession of pot in Saudi Arabia results in amputation of one ear and a prison sentence of no less than four years." I am completely making this up, under the diffuse influence of the movie *Midnight Express*, which I saw last year.

Seung's eyes widen. "No! How do you know that?"

"Read it in a book by a French journalist who got arrested there."

"Did he get his ear hacked off?"

"No. The French government intervened, and he got some help from a beautiful Saudi woman who turned out to be an undercover agent for the U.S."

We smoke in silence, occasionally taking slugs from my flask. As soon as the joint is spent, Seung lights up another. "I planned to cut back this year," he says, "but it didn't happen."

"Cut back on weed? Why bother?"

"Aviva. She didn't like it."

Aviva. I've forgotten about her, truly I have. Just for this brief time she's been taken out of the equation between Seung and me; we've simply been two guys lying on the bank, sharing weed and conversation in the dusk. My throat tightens up and I feel a pressure on my heart.

"She doesn't smoke?" I ask, for something to say.

"She'd like to," he replies, without elaborating.

I glance at my watch. It's 7:53 PM, two hours and seven minutes until check-in. One week and six days until graduation. *My* graduation, anyway. *If* I graduate. It's starting to make me nervous, being out here with Seung when he's so messed up. If he starts getting strange on me, I can't be babysitting him or shepherding him home. I can't get implicated.

I stand up, to tell Seung I'm heading out, but my head is heavy as a bowling ball and I weave for a moment, unable to speak. I pray I'm going to pass muster with Mr. Glass and his clipboard. Mr. Glass doesn't go out of his way to catch kids breaking the rules, but if you don't even have the decency to try to fool him, he figures he has to take action. I sit down again and rest my head on my knees. When I feel steadier—it's several minutes later, not a peep from Seung—I scrabble around in my knapsack. There's a candy bar in there and a flashlight. Both are good, but finding the flashlight fills me with special relief. By some pot-induced logic, its presence seems, for now, to solve the dilemma of check-in. I can relax; things are going to be okay. I settle myself, aware that I have many problems that the flashlight does not solve, but I can't remember precisely what they are.

"Shit, I just noticed your ring," Seung says.

"This?" I say. I snatch my hand from his view. "It's just a joke, man. My dad bought it for me."

He beckons me to show it to him, gets his face close to it and peers at the inscription. "*Gnaritas et Patientia*. Rah rah."

"Yeah. Dad was class of '44."

"No shit."

"No shit. And his dad was class of '13. And *his* dad . . . you get the idea."

"Oh, man, son of class of '44, great-grandson of Class of Nineteenth Century. That's almost worse than being son of Korean PhD and his doctor wife."

I am surprised that he understands this.

I slip off the ring and hand it to him.

"I've never actually touched one of those things," Seung tells me. "Detweiler had one but he kept it in some sort of Kryptonite box." He can't get it onto his ring finger—his fingers are so broad and thick-jointed—so he slides it onto his pinky. I notice the blisters on the thumb and index fingers of his hand.

The distortion and heavy-headedness are passing out of me in a series of waves. I'm beginning to trust my faculties again.

"You'll give it to your own son one day," Seung tells me.

"I doubt that."

He flexes his fingers, staring at the seal of the ring. "Bruce Bennett-Jones," he muses. "Bruce Bennett-Jones. I've wasted my fucking life."

"Wasted your life?" I laugh. "Come on, Jung. You'll go home, go to Jordan High, and you'll be in college by the winter if you don't do anything seriously boneheaded."

He isn't even paying attention to me. "I've lost the respect of my parents," he says very calmly, clenching and unclenching his fist. "I've lost my girlfriend. I've pissed away forty thousand dollars my parents spent to send me here. I've pissed away my self-respect."

He's lost his girlfriend?

He knocks himself on the head a couple of times and I can't tell if he's really hurting himself or not. It doesn't look good.

"I tried, Bennett-Jones. I tried so fucking hard."

"Come on, Jung. Quit that." I'm trying to decide if he could really mean what he seems to mean: that he and Aviva have broken up. What could have led to that? It's impossible to take in. They are famous, they are the sexual and romantic templates for the rest of us.

"Aviva . . ?" I croak.

"I've destroyed her. I've *humiliated* her," he says. "I'm not a man."

I figure he's just talking crazy—weed talk. I can't speak her name again; it will sear me. "Maybe she'll change her mind," I say clumsily. "Girls are like that. Maybe tomorrow she'll want you back."

"She won't want me back. You don't know her."

I stare at him, unable to reply. Because I do know her. I've imagined every part of her: her body, her thoughts, the conversations she has with her friends, with her brother and father and mother, the things she says to him, Seung, the books she reads and the fantasies that make her touch herself. I know the look of the apartment she's grown up in and the park near her old high school and the arrogant marginalia she scribbles in her schoolbooks. "You're right," I say finally. "She won't go back to you."

He studies me. Then he nods, as if he understands something finally: who I am, what my relation to him is. For the first time he recognizes that we're in competition, that once, in our childhoods, I was more than he was, and that now, because of what has happened, I'm going to be the stronger once again.

Seung pitches a stone into the water.

"I cheated on her once," he says. "Over spring vacation. A girl in Jordan."

I feel a rush of indignation on Aviva's behalf. The bastard. "Why?"

"Why?" he looks momentarily puzzled. "I had to."

Something unlocks in me. I intuit something—I couldn't have put it in words at the time. No, I pieced things together only later. Still, there is something I realize I am going to say, that perhaps I've been meaning to say all along, from the very beginning, from the first time I ever saw Seung and Aviva together on the Weld common room couch. My words appear to me full-bloomed and with such vividness that as far as I am concerned they are the truth and not a lie. I feel steady and very strong. I stand up, stretch my arms as if I could reach up and grab the moon.

"You know," I say, "I wasn't going to tell you this, but since you're leaving now and you've broken up with her, I think you ought to know. I fucked her, Jung. It was a while ago, back in the winter. Remember the Kent swim tournament, your team stayed overnight? Then."

I don't even notice him getting to his feet. All at once he's right up close to me, big and broad, and I think he's going to take a swing at me. I stand my ground. Somehow I know that, no matter what he does, he can't hurt me. I could bleed to death right here and I've still won.

"Bennett-Jones, don't mess with me over something like that."

"I'm not messing with you. It's the truth. There was a dance that night, right? At Pepperdine dorm. She was there with no one to dance with. Or everyone to dance with. We went for a walk along the river and then we went to her room."

Seung grabs me by the shirt. His face is dark, dark. "Why would you say this to me, man? You're sitting here sharing my weed, we're talking together . . . why do you want to shit on me?"

"I'm trying to protect you. I don't want you to be all broken up about her. You should know the truth."

"You're a shit-sucking liar."

"She has a purple bra," I say. "A weird color, like a grape lollipop. It's got a little thingy in the center, like an embroidered flower or something, with the letter *P* on it."

Seung draws back his fist, and I close my eyes. But when I open them he's already past me and moving toward the water. "Tell me more!" he shouts. His back is to me. "Say it louder!" I watch as he pulls off his shirt. I still don't know why he did that—pulled off his shirt, I mean. It was already wet. The shirt was green—I would have reason to remember that later. So I tell him more, I say it louder. I raise my voice, so he'll catch every word. I tell him how she gripped me with her thighs, I describe the sounds that came from her, and now I'm telling him it wasn't just once, we did it a few times, once in the wardrobe room at the Dramat, I knelt above her, and . . .

Seung is in the water now, swimming toward the opposite bank, strong, furious strokes. He flips under and starts back. Back and forth between the banks he goes, wearing out his rage. I'm shouting now, and my story is the story of all the things I wish I had done, of places I touched Aviva and the feel of her skin and the purr of her voice, and, gradually, my anger turns to tenderness, and I describe not fucking but making love; I describe playfulness and appreciation, and in doing so I lose control over my tale, become implausible. I describe encounters that never could have happened, the two of us on a beach in California, a visit Aviva made to New Jersey (we made love quietly while my mother bumbled around the kitchen), but Seung can no longer hear me anyway, or can hear only fragments; the crashing of his arms and the rushing of the water past him seals his ears. And now it hits him—I see this in my mind's eye—the lysergic acid, which I learned about only later, metabolizes, and the Bog sparks with light, tiny winking bits of living energy that dance on the surface of the water. Seung's breathing slows until it is as thick and slow as the water around him seems to be. But this thickened substance does not hamper him, it cradles him, and Seung sees that there's no one to blame. He forgets there is such a thing as blame. The black trees bend and touch the skin of the Bog, which is a breathing skin, full of mouths sucking in and releasing oxygen, an unending cycle of breath and life. Seung is treading water, and he ducks down under the skin to breathe better, to breathe in this unending source of breath.

I'm on the bank, still mouthing my story, feeling the dark close in as the sun makes its last descent behind the trees. One minute Seung is treading water; the next moment I don't see him anymore. I think he's making an underwater turn and starting back toward the bank. When he reaches me perhaps he'll knock me down; perhaps he'll beat me to a pulp. That would be all right. I'm ready for it. I wait to see his shape rise out of the water. But the difference between the sky and the water is blurred by the darkness and I can't tell where he is. After a while I begin to think he's fucking around with me. He's crouching in the brush on the other side of the Bog, waiting for me to get worried. Waiting for me to start walking the bank looking for him, and in the darkness he'll leap out and yank my fucking head off. Again, the thought of being hurt by Seung doesn't bother me so much, but the thought of him in the shadows, manipulating me, silently laughing at me, does. I won't play his game. I'll just turn and go. It must be getting close to check-in time anyway. But I can't leave. I am, in spite of myself, growing anxious. I reach for my flashlight and point it toward the water; its weak beam illuminates nothing. I call Seung's name. Come on, Jung, I say. Don't be crazy. Come out. Come on back. I wave the flashlight around.

I don't know how much time passes. I start to think that maybe the pot has altered my sense of duration, that Seung has been out of view only a few seconds. I call again, louder this time. Now I am sure that time is passing. It finally occurs to me to look at my watch. Eight forty. But that doesn't tell me anything. I don't know what time it was when I lost sight of his black hair skimming the water. I squat down on the ground and try to breathe. Either Seung is hiding in the woods right now or he's treading water very quietly in a darkened spot that I can't see. I stand up again and shout out that he's a motherfucker, that I was only telling him the truth, that I'm leaving now. My voice is unsteady. I take Seung's discarded shirt and sneakers and I throw them into a mucky stretch of bank where the woods come thickly right up to the water.

"Have fun walking back!" I shout. As I leave the Bog behind I dwell on the image of Seung making his way to campus barefoot, shirtless, slapped at by dark branches. His punishment for scaring me, playing with me. Wonder how that will look, Jung, you arriving at Mr. Glass's door soaking wet, bedraggled, obviously stoned. Guess they can't do anything more to you now, though, can they?

Do I believe all of this bitter, gloating talk that keeps me company as I head back toward civilization? Do I believe Seung's feet are on the ground?

They are not. He's descending now, going deep as I zigzag this way and that until I find the path out. For a minute, ninety seconds perhaps, Seung's body instinctively struggles against the liquid filling his lungs, but then, abruptly, the fear disappears. He's dissolving into the living, breathing substance of the water. There are no obstacles. He's nobody's son, nobody's lover. Fleetingly he catches sight of Aviva's face, not Aviva herself but an image of her, an image captured in a mirror, a broken shard, that drifts past and slowly sinks below him. He is a broken shard, too; they are both shards descending in a sea of shards: meaningless, glittering, lovely, dangerous; this is the world's design and he accepts it as he goes down.

54

They start the search for Seung around ten thirty. Sterne checks in at ten and realizes that Seung isn't in their room. He stops by Giddings's room, but Giddings hasn't seen Seung since their dinner. The two head down to Mr. Glass's apartment, thinking maybe Seung slipped in to talk with the teacher. Mr. Glass tells them Seung checked in shortly after seven. He asks them to find their friend and report back to him.

The two boys inspect the bathroom on each floor, calling sharply. By ten twenty Giddings is at my door, asking questions. David is hunched over his biology book, ignoring me. He waited forty-five minutes at our rendezvous spot and then headed to the library. I told him I chickened out and went into town for ice cream. The expensive cognac is now hidden in a suitcase at the back of his closet. I told him his underwear drawer was a stupid place to keep it.

You can hear Giddings and Sterne knocking on other doors, low conversations.

At ten forty Mr. Glass calls an emergency dorm meeting and says that Seung is missing. He's already phoned the Dean of Students, who in turn has notified security. There isn't a whole lot they can do in the darkness. My lower year, there was a kid who disappeared before his disciplinary hearing—he'd been caught smoking pot. One evening he never showed up for check-in, but the next morning, he was back, cold and subdued after a night alone in the woods. He'd just flipped out temporarily, scared of what was coming. But Seung's already been kicked out; what would be the point in running off? Might he be frightened to return home to his parents? Sterne and Giddings emphatically say no to this conjecture. Seung is the type to face up to things, to tough them out. He wouldn't run from his folks. And then the room falls silent, as everybody thinks of the same alternative at the same time. Seung has crept into one of the closed buildings and found some way to hang or stab or gas himself. Mr. Glass waits, in case someone possesses some hint, some clue. . . . No one does.

Finally, Mr. Glass tells us all to get some sleep, but I doubt many of us do. I don't. I lie in bed and when a truck goes past with blazing headlights I instantly wonder if it's going out to search the Bog. Then I remind myself that there are hundreds of places to search, and no reason anyone should think of the Bog in particular. Besides, it's nighttime; they wouldn't be going to the Bog at night. Be quiet, I tell myself, don't worry, just be patient. Seung could be walking back to Weld right now, cutting his feet on protruding tree roots, cursing me for hiding his shoes.

But Seung doesn't return that night, and he doesn't return the next day. The search goes on, and I watch David for signs that he connects my failure to meet him with Seung's disappearance. The thought doesn't appear to have entered his mind. I keep myself distracted with the hypothesis that Seung slept in the woods and then hitchhiked to the nearest bus station. But without shoes, without money? And to go where? By the end of the first day my speculations are getting frantic and frankly absurd. That night, during a few hours of sleep, I dream of Seung lying in a water-drenched coffin, a fat fishing hook through his mouth, my class ring—my ring!—on one grotesquely oversized pinky, and I wake knowing he is dead. And that I will be punished. The ring was never inscribed, but I am convinced that if the searchers find it, they'll eventually find me.

The police are a visible presence on campus, not just the Auburn PD but the county police too. Every student knows a different part of the story. Some parts you can get by buttonholing faculty who are willing to talk (Mr. Glass, for the most part, is), some by reading the local newspaper, the *Auburn Banner*. The police send out missing-person bulletins to the two local cab companies and Greyhound and Amtrak. They talk at length to Giddings, who eventually breaks down and admits to having given Seung two tabs of acid. Sterne refuses to confirm this or to say anything at all but that the three of them had dinner together and that Seung did not seem depressed and that he had given no indication in recent weeks that flight or suicide was on his mind. The waitress at Waterlilies reports that all three of the boys seemed intoxicated; one of them, she can't remember which, broke a glass. Giddings is sent home where, for almost a year, he works a job at a local record store and studies for his high school equivalency exam. He is scheduled to appear in New Hampshire court on felony charges of distributing a Schedule I substance, but at some point— so the grapevine reports—the charges are dropped. I once heard that Giddings eventually went to medical school. Sterne does something in finance out in LA.

On the third day, having had no luck tracing Seung to another location, the police step up their search of the Auburn grounds. It is not they but a student, a kid hanging out with a few friends at the Bog after finals one afternoon, who notices something in the woods near the bank, a green slightly different from the green of the foliage, something that could be a piece of clothing. It proves in fact to be a shirt, and there's a pair of sneakers lying nearby. The police have checked the Bog before but now they come back and bag the objects, and Seung's friends confirm that he wore a green shirt when they went out to dinner that night. The fourth day is the one on which the body is brought up. Since then I've learned what a human being looks like when he's been four days drowned. I won't go into detail here about the bloating and the discoloration, the start of decomposition. It would have been awful to behold. I force myself to envision the details now, but I avoided them then, and even after the search ended and the mystery was resolved, there was a part of me that did not believe Seung was dead. For someone to be dead, you need to have a dead body, and the last I'd seen of Seung was his strong arms in motion as he plowed through the dark water, lit up with pain and rage.

My class ring never comes into the story at all. It must have been found on Seung—naturally I did not ask—but no one connected it with me; how could they have?

Someone has died, but certain things cannot be altered. There have to be finals and graduation for everyone who is still alive. The finals schedule is shifted and compressed to leave time for special services at the Academy church. Mr. Bonney, the chaplain, holds open houses at his apartment for students who want to come and mourn and talk. Rumors circulate: Seung's pants had stones in the pockets; Seung slashed his wrists before he entered the water. A widely voiced opinion has it that Seung was essentially killed by the administration, by its brutal suppression of, its hatred of, the natural act of sex. People forget how much they disliked Seung and Aviva's exhibitionism, how much they resented their pleasures. There is talk of staging a protest during graduation ceremonies. No one has ever heard of any sort of campus protest, not even in the old hippie days, and no one knows quite how to go about it. Some students argue that disrupting the ceremonies would be unfair to parents and that graduation should be a day of celebration. The truth is that everyone is so relieved and delighted to be successfully graduating that there isn't much traction for the protest.

What is odd is the coexistence of a mood of disbelief and horror and the absolute forgetfulness that comes with worrying about test results, packing up, dressing up, and the arrival of family. Graduation takes place on a warm and cloudy June Sunday, on a platform set up in front of the Assembly Building. We seniors sit in folding chairs facing the platform, in alphabetical order, while the underclassmen sit behind us and the parents in chairs set up at the sides, except for Dak-ho Jung, who occupies the seat that would have been his son's and who will be accepting Seung's diploma for him. They are apparently giving Seung one after all. Seung's father has yet to receive the autopsy report, which will tell him that his son had a potent combination of alcohol and THC and lysergic acid in his system when he died. I look around to identify where my parents are located—I am hoping they can't readily see me—and my eyes pass over Aviva, who is on the other side of the aisle and a few rows behind me with the other uppers. She stares at the ground, as if she intends never to look straight at anything again.

I grasp the proffered diploma in my left hand while allowing the principal to pump my right, and then it is all over, these four years of study and play and fear and resentment and wanting, wanting, wanting. There's an old Auburn tradition of clapping softly for each classmate as the procession begins, increasing the volume as the middle of the alphabet is reached, then drowning out the final names with stamping and hollering and general lunacy. But today nobody makes noise. We watch Seung's father as he gets up with his row of students and gradually makes his way to the podium. He is no taller than Jonathan Joyce-Haverford ahead of him or Andrea Kallas behind. No one can remove his eyes from the drab brown jacket Mr. Jung wears or the pants that puddle over his neatly polished black shoes. His face betrays no expression, but students begin to cry quietly as he moves closer to the stage and finally mounts the steps to take the diploma. He nods stiffly when he receives it. I cry, too, believe me. I can't help it, when people are weeping all around me, and, guided by the gaze of others, I seek out Seung's mother and brother in the parents' rows. I truly miss Seung then; his absence hurts me and seems inconceivable. Inconceivable that a living person should be snuffed out. I turn to look at Aviva again, wondering how she is taking all this. She is dry-eyed, silent, still staring into the grass.

After the last name is called and the awards are given and our commencement speaker has finished, the clouds shift and sunlight spears down into the crowd. People put on sunglasses and begin to drift toward the graduation picnic. Someone hovers near me and I realize it is Seung's mother. She is short, plump, solid. Her hair is pulled back in a simple bun. She is dressed in a dark suit and carries a small dark purse. She looks at me curiously. I think she recognizes me from around Jordan but can't quite place me. I can't bear to hold her gaze, and I make sure, as I put a hamburger and chips and a couple of brownies on my plate (I always have an appetite; nothing ever stops my appetite), to stay far away from wherever the Jung family happens to be.

55

A kid named Charlie Bradley has a family farm—hay, goats, and Christmas trees—about twenty miles northwest of Portsmouth, and he's hosting a big graduation party there. Carlyle and Lena urge Aviva to go, even though neither of them will be able to join her. Carlyle's parents have booked her ticket to Dulles for the evening of graduation, precisely so that she won't attend any parties, and Lena has to rush home for a state piano competition. Aviva—her friends say—needs to be around other people, especially Seung's buddies. They don't know that Aviva broke things off with Seung the night he died, that when she sees Sterne and Giddings and the others all she can think of is that she murdered their friend. Yet she lets them be good to her; she can't bear for them or anyone to know the truth, what she did and what she said. They take their meals with her and walk her to her finals, and Giddings gives her Seung's copy of *The Doors of Perception*, filled with his notes. There's been talk of Charlie Bradley canceling the party because of what happened, but in the end people agree that Seung, if he could pronounce on the matter, would want everybody to have a kick-ass celebration.

Aviva doesn't want to go to the party. She doesn't want to go anywhere. During finals she mostly stayed in her room, studying for long hours next to her roommate. Carlyle has invited her to stay at her home in Virginia for a couple of weeks, but Aviva can't imagine being in the midst of someone else's family life, having to eat their food and join their conversations. She can't bear the idea of being *watched*, studied for signs of grief and distress, or their absence. On the other hand, she dreads the thought of returning to Chicago and that deeply silent apartment with its creeping shabbiness, where even the presence of Marshall seems no safeguard against a slow, clotting despair.

So she says yes to the party.

No one is officially invited to Charlie's party; everybody just knows about it. I convince David Yee to come with me. I want a night of darkness and chaos, of getting openly trashed. I figure he'll have forgiven me by now, and it seems he has. To my relief, Lisa has no interest in joining me. We say good-bye as she gets into her parents' car for the drive home to Brookline, neither of us making any noises about a summer meeting or even exchanging letters. We are both utterly content to be rid of each other.

Asking around, I find a ride with a day student I hardly know. When he and David and I get to Charlie's place around 9:00 PM, the party is in full swing. There's a half moon low in the sky and it's very dark outside the farmhouse proper. People wander with bottles in their hands, beer or whiskey, searching out private spots to talk, drink, screw. In the basement of the big house, near shelves holding a few onions and potatoes, there is a Ping-Pong table and an enormous freezer and refrigerator. The fridge holds beer and the freezer vodka, along with huge hunks of meat wrapped in white paper. Scattered across a stainless-steel table are open bags of chips and pretzels.

I play Ping-Pong for a while with David and then go out to get some air. There are hayfields behind the house, an empty structure that someone claims is an old chicken coop, and, farther away, an archery range with targets pinned to bales. I'm wondering if Aviva is here tonight. After Seung's body was found, she left Auburn for a couple of days; a cousin or aunt from Connecticut drove up to collect her. When she came back we all studied her, looking for something—we weren't sure what. She had some dark knowledge inside of her, something vast and slumbering that might shoot quills at us if we got too close. From the outside, though, Aviva appeared more or less the same as always, or at least the same as she'd come to look over the course of the year: thin, pale, a little less bold in her carriage. But it was hard to get a handle on her. Seung's crowd closed around her, protecting her, hiding her from curious eyes.

They are with her now. I've circled back to the farmhouse and see her walking in my direction, flanked by

Sterne and Giddings and some of their Weld hangers-on. There's something loose but careful in her walk that makes me think she might be drunk. That would be interesting— a drunk Aviva. I'm not going to be able to get close to her, though, so I bushwhack into the fields until I come across a group spread out on blankets, drinking and nodding to a boom box blaring the Allman Brothers. It isn't my kind of music, but it's loud, loud enough that I can get swamped by the noise, lose track of the outside world for a while. I lie down on my back and close my eyes. Someone puts a beer in my hand.

Time goes by. It must be about an hour, because I remember the Allman Brothers finishing and then both sides of *Aqualung* being played. I'm liking this little pocket of existence, where people come and go every so often, unspoken to, unmolested. I'm inclined never to leave. But some instinct makes me open my eyes just in time to see David Yee pass by in the company of some girl, looks like a lower maybe, a tiny little thing who will be sorry later when she figures out what a dork she's attached herself to. *Well, well, David*, I think. Somebody in the pile of bodies finally speaks, commenting slurringly that "they" are setting off firecrackers at the archery range, and when I listen I can hear the sharp spattering sound. I get up, take a swig of Heineken, and leave the bottle with someone else.

I haven't gotten far when I see Aviva on the stoop of the chicken house. She's with Cort, of all people. I don't think the two of them have ever spoken in their lives. I wonder where Seung's crowd went. They wouldn't have left her; she must have separated herself from them. She's got her eyes closed and Cort's arm is draped around her. *For chrissakes, Cort,* I think. *You're a faggot!* Aviva is wearing a long skirt and an oversized oxford that in the light of the bulb fixed above the stoop seems to be either white or pale blue. It was Seung's shirt, maybe. I am sure it was Seung's. I go cold looking at it. It is as if Aviva has draped Seung's dead body around her shoulders. Does no one else notice this? Does it make no one else recoil?

Cort greets me drunkenly. Aviva raises her head from his shoulder and blinks at me indifferently. Though this doesn't amount to much of an invitation, I crouch down opposite them. It's a humid but bug-free night.

"Aviva's going to Europe," Cort tells me.

"Oh."

"With Lena," Aviva adds unexpectedly. Her eyes close again. "Two months, Eurail Pass, everything. My father told me about the tickets this morning."

"That must be nice," I say, "to have a father who gives you tickets to Europe."

"I was supposed to find a job this summer. And see a shrink. But Lena's aunt called my mother and my mother called my father. It'll be cheaper than an actual shrink—I'm sure that's what convinced my dad."

"Come on, you don't know that," I say.

"Traveling will be good for you," Cort tells her soothingly. I wonder when he developed such a confident sense of Aviva's psychological needs. I despise the sound of her name in his mouth. *Aviva.* I believe he has no right.

"Cort will be taking math this summer," I inform her. "University of Maryland only agreed to take him provisionally. No hittee grade level, no gettee in."

"Right, Bennett-Jones. I'll be haunted all my life by the shame." He lifts a flat bottle to his mouth, takes a swig, passes it to Aviva. She hesitates, then puts her narrow, fragile-looking fingers around it.

"Cort." All three of us look up. No one heard Voss approach, and now he looms above us. His shirt is unbuttoned to midchest; he's sweating exhibitionistically. His feet are planted like a man expecting a fight.

Cort disentangles himself from Aviva and struggles upright. "Hey, man."

"Billy Lavery is shooting a Winchester rifle out there. I want to check it out."

"He has a gun?" Aviva asks. She stands, too, batting a leaf out of her hair.

"Bradley's folks have a whole room full of guns and rifles and even some Civil War shit, but it's fricking triple-locked. This one, though, Charlie found in the basement."

"It's dark," Aviva says. Her hands are on her hips. She seems less drunk now.

"Billy's got a lantern. *Cort.*"

"Coming, for fuck's sake."

"Someone could get hurt," insists Aviva.

"No one's going to get hurt," says Voss. "Billy isn't stupid."

"Don't be such a thickheaded dick," says Cort. "Think of what Aviva's been through, man."

Voss looks briefly at his sneakers. "Billy's had only, like, two beers," he says. "And Charlie isn't going to let anyone else shoot."

He strides off in the direction of the archery range. Cort hurries to join him.

"Idiots," comments Aviva.

She looks around, as if distressed to find herself all alone, as if I am not still crouched there a few feet from her. The bulb light makes the buttons of her shirt gleam, and I try again to figure out what color it is. I'm regretting giving away that beer I had.

"I wish I hadn't come," Aviva says.

She turns and walks after Cort and Voss. I scramble up to follow.

She must hear my steps, but she doesn't speed up or tell me to go away. In a moment I've caught up. She doesn't acknowledge my presence.

"I'm sorry," I say. I'm out of breath, from nerves. "I'm sorry about Seung." Just now, I *am* sorry. I'm sorry about everything. I want things to be better for her. I want her to stop looking so depleted and vulnerable.

"All right," she says. "Thanks."

She increases her pace; apparently, she's done with the conversation. But a few moments later, she stops short and makes an impatient gesture. "What do you want?" she asks.

"It must be terrible," I say. I mean nothing in particular by this. I just need to say sentences to her. They form themselves without my thought or involvement. I need her to acknowledge me.

Her lips are closed, contemptuous. "It's not terrible," she says. "It's not anything. It's nothing, *nothing*."

I can't truly hear her. I keep talking. "Of course I can't really know what it's like when someone you care about dies. I can't really know what . . ."

"I don't feel *anything*," she interrupts. "Do you get that? Does anybody get that? I'm cold. I'm cold all the way through. There's something missing in me, just like I always thought."

"It's not true," I say.

I don't see it coming. Her hand strikes me across the face. She looks surprised. She clutches the hand with the other one and shuts her eyes. "What the fuck do you know?" she says.

"Okay, okay," I say. I feel, with alarm, that tears are rising to my eyes. I beg them to stay away. The skin around my left eye prickles.

"Okay," I repeat. I believe that I'm backing away from her; I even see myself turning toward the farmhouse, moving back toward the big porch and the lights. But clearly I don't do this, because I find I am on my knees, my arms around her legs, my head against her belly, weeping. Her belly is flat, a little bony, but very soft too. Her hand comes down and rests on my head.

"Please," I say. "Please."

I reach up and undo the bottom button of her long shirt—Seung's shirt. Then the next button. I want to put my cheek against her and tangle in the warm metal of her necklaces and feel the warmed skin beneath. Then I realize it's not her I need to be naked but me. I turn my shaking hands to myself. I pull off my shirt and kneel there with my short, fleshy chest, my ugliness exposed.

There's the report of a gun going off, then cheers. I rise and take Aviva's hand and lead her into the hayfield. We lie down on the ground, breaking the stalks under us, and kiss. Her mouth is warm and tastes of rum. She does not make a sound but I feel her breathing slow and thicken, and, just as I've imagined so many times, she raises her arms around me. Her mouth is a tunnel I can get lost in. I reach down and feel the whole length of her—her own intimate shape, plane and slope, curve and bone. She's shivering. I spread my shirt on top of her, on top of the man's shirt she's already wearing. I unbuckle myself, pull off my jeans and underpants. She sits up, clutching my shirt, waiting. Her skirt is pushed up above satiny-looking panties. I don't know if I can bear it anymore. My cock is going to split out of its skin, break open like a fruit. For a moment the old violence comes up in me and I feel as if I could maul her in my desperation to have her to myself. But I hold back, I hold back. She lets me lower myself onto her and stroke her; I can feel her chest and belly soften underneath me and yet she keeps her legs rigid. I stop. I ask her if I should go on.

—Yes.

She sounds far away. I kiss her again, and again she feels warm and receptive, but then she turns her mouth away as if to say, Get on with it. I nudge her apart as best I can and she squirms to accommodate me. I push in slightly; she's wet but tight. Then with pent-up impatience I push again, harder, and she cries out sharply.

I fall back on my knees, apologizing. She lifts her head, tries to smile. "It's okay," she says. I know it's all going wrong but I can't stop now, my greed and joy send me on. I push in again, more gently this time. She is quiet now, very still. I feel as if I am moving in a horrific emptiness. I thrust in once more, and she makes a little *ah!*—of pleasure or discomfort I can't tell—and then, all at once, all happiness and will drain from me and I pull out, panting, my cock throbbing in painful protest.

Aviva sits up, her eyes wide. "No," she says. "Don't stop."

I crawl away from her, let the hay close behind me. And there, with my back to her, I tug and yank at myself until— it doesn't take long—I spill. I wipe myself off, cry quickly and quietly, rub my eyes with my forearm. Everything is humid, sticky, soiled.

When I come back to our spot, she's fled. My shirt and jeans and underpants lie here and there on the ground. I gather them up and my hands find something else: a ring, at least it feels so in the darkness, smooth and bumpy. I pull my clothes on slowly, slip my find into my pocket, spit to get the taste of something out of my mouth. I walk dizzily toward the farmhouse, stopping once to piss in the weeds, and, after grabbing a fresh beer from the cooler, seek out a dark spot against the back wall outside, where few people see me or speak to me for the rest of the evening. At some point I fall asleep, and I don't wake until someone shakes me by the shoulders. It's the day student, who has been decent enough not to leave without me and is prepared to drop me and David at the Greyhound station in Portsmouth as promised. David is wearing a shit-eating grin. He must have gotten somewhere with that lower girl.

In the light of the bus station, as we wait for the first of the day's buses to Boston, I examine Aviva's ring, gold with little ruby chips, narrower at the bottom than at the setting, as delicate as she is. I lost a ring to Seung and from Aviva I gained one. I slip it back into my pocket.

Many hours later, in my parents' home, disheveled, still hungover, I step into the shower to rid myself of the crud and grime of the previous evening, and I see the dried blood on my penis. It takes me a minute to realize that's what it is. Aviva was starting her period, is what I think at first. Could that be right? Maybe that's why she was so ambivalent, so tense. Still, I can't help feeling that it's the blood of a wounding, an assault. I can't make sense of it all—this thing I wanted so much to do, waited to do, then fled from again. What is its meaning to me now? When I was inside of her I thought of Seung stretched out on his back at the Bog, his head in the dirt, that weed smile on his lips, still alive, breathing, blood pumping throughout his veins and valves. "The shape of a pull toy," he'd said of a THC molecule. I'd thought of that, pressing into Aviva, moving in and out, until, looking at her face, so stricken and impoverished, I couldn't go on.

And now, as the hot water courses over me, I make a different set of connections. I remember Aviva's startled cry, so like Lisa Flood's the first time I entered her. I think of Seung at the Bog saying that he'd failed, that he'd had to cheat on Aviva, that he wasn't a man, and these things mix together with other, less formed thoughts, and all at once I know: my God, Aviva, the great Auburn slut, had been a virgin.

56

So I was her first then? But I felt no triumph as the days and the weeks passed, rather that my crime against Aviva had doubled, and so had my responsibility toward her. I recognized myself now as someone filled with ugly and perhaps uncontrollable impulses. Who knew what I might do next? I might break a window and leap past the debris to steal stereo equipment or diamonds. I might attack someone, unprovoked, in the street. I was drinking a lot, and in truth that made me too stupid and uncoordinated to do anyone much harm. But it did not prevent certain images from appearing before me over and over: Seung's body sunk at the bottom of the Bog, drifting and bloated; a ring—*Gnaritas et Patientia*—manacling one swollen finger. I thought of confessing to the Dean of Students or the police, and could not convince myself to do it. It's not that I believed I could be charged with Seung's death—it would fall short of that—but in the eyes of the world the distinction would be technical. I knew what I knew: Aviva and I together had snuffed Seung out. I had no courage. Evenings, in bed, I put my face to my knees and rocked fast, using the motion to keep my mind blank.

57

David Yee and I weren't the only ones from Charlie Bradley's party at the Greyhound station that early morning, waiting for the sun to rise and for the buses that would take us toward our homes. There were others, too, as rumpled and night-stained as we were. Among them was Aviva. Did she come in before me or afterward? I never saw her enter. I was sitting with my head hanging somewhere between my chest and my feet. David, entirely sober and his polo shirt somehow still crisp and clean, was reading the previous Sunday's *New York Times*. I was thirsty and headed toward the bathroom in the hope that the sink worked and I could get a few swallows of water. I saw a shape from the corner of my eye, well across the room, but I knew it as if it were the shape of a mother or a sister. For a moment I was terrified; in my mixed-up consciousness, I had the idea that I'd killed Aviva the night before and yet here she was, back from the dead to

accuse me. Adrenaline spun me from my path to the bathroom back toward my seat. After resettling myself gingerly I
stole another look, thinking that Aviva might have vanished
by now, might have been merely a hangover-induced appa-
rition. But there she was. I touched the ring in my pocket
and turned it and turned it. I spoke silently to myself until I
once more believed that the girl sitting on the opposite side
of the room by the broken snack dispenser was an ordinary
girl, an ordinary living girl whom I had tried to love in the
grass last night until I'd seen that I could not reach her and
did not deserve to reach her. David read the paper and occasionally looked up at me for an excessively long moment,
clearly wanting to be asked about his evening.

Something squawked over the loudspeaker, an unintel-
ligible crackle. I checked my watch: it was still too early
for the bus I would ride, with one transfer, all the way to
New York City. I felt rather than saw Aviva rise, and as she
passed I took her inventory: brown peasant skirt, oversized oxford—I finally could plainly see its color as pale
blue—chunky brown clogs. No earrings, only two necklaces—why? A knapsack, apparently holding very little, for
it drooped limply off one shoulder. She did not turn to look
at me, and although I'd in no way expected that she would,
the feeling of absence as she passed was like a dark wind. I
snatched at her scent: stale booze, sleep, some remnant of
the clean outdoors. I stood and stumbled after her, calling
to her to wait. She turned, and her eyes frightened me: they
were empty, without expectation or irritation. They seemed

almost blind. I opened my fist, saw her register the little ruby ring lying in my hand. A spark fired briefly into those eyes. She reached out and took the ring, her cold fingertips brushing the lifelines on my palm. I longed to close my hand upon hers, just for a moment, by way of apology, by way of explaining that I would always love her, but I resisted, and I can say now that nothing in my life since has ever been as difficult as that self-control.

"Thank you," she said hoarsely. Her eyes did not meet mine again.

Through the smeared glass door of the bus depot I watched Aviva cross onto the asphalt lane where her bus idled, juddering erratically. I saw her small form rise one step and then two into the dark interior. She would never come back to Auburn. I don't know if she had already made that decision as I sat there, noting her exchange with the driver—she said something, and then he said something. People brought it up from time to time over that next year, as they made their college visits from Auburn—remember Aviva Rossner, she didn't return. Aviva nodded at the driver and turned toward the long tunnel of seats and then she disappeared behind the tinted glass.

ACKNOWLEDGEMENTS

Deep thanks to my agent, Anna Stein, and my editor, Tony Perez, each of whom has given so much to this book, and whose loyalty I prize. Thanks also to Anna's assistant John McElwee and to the dynamic Nanci McCloskey, Rob Spillman, Diane Chonette, Jakob Vala, Anne Horowitz, and the rest of the amazing crew at Tin House Books, as wonderful a home as an author could hope for.

Jim Ruland, Jane Avrich, and Joanne Fisher read the manuscript and gave invaluable feedback, while "the Thursday group" of Therese Eiben, Lynn Schmeidler, Joanne Fisher (again), and Philip Moustakis helped with tune-ups. So did Kirsten Menger-Anderson.

Harold Brown offered me carte blanche and tour-guide services on a research trip, while Peter Greer and the late David Thomas responded to queries about boarding school life. John Casey explained crew; Daniel Gesmer got me up to speed on skateboarding. John Kim, Dot Bowe, and Caryn Bowe answered various oddball questions. Christine Schutt illuminated the big picture.

Julia Bogardus and Susan Lane: Just because you helped with material that didn't end up making it into *The Virgins* doesn't mean you didn't help. My fault, not yours. Same goes for the late, warm-hearted Louis E. Catron.

My pals at Zoetrope Virtual Studio—too many to name, but I want to offer special appreciation to Mary Akers, Roy Kesey, Pia Z. Ehrhardt, Alicia Gifford, Myfanwy Collins, Ellen Meister, Cliff Garstang, Darlin Neal, Len Joy, Marko Fong, Jim Tomlinson, Anne Elliott, and Mary Lynn Reed—keep me feeling that the writer's life is not only survivable but a privilege.

Claudia Putnam and Elena Sigman have always shared the passion and listened to the complaints.

The Seasoned Moms—you know who you are—maintain my balance so I can put the words on the page.

No copy question is too minor for Phyliss Greenberg to deal with at the eleventh hour, and my husband, Jonathan Ratner, is also a crack pro bono proofreader.

Kathy Melillo: Thanks for making everything run smoothly while I was upstairs.

It feels corny to say it, but my mother, Patricia Erens, always believed I really was a writer—or at least she did a good job of hiding any doubts. It's time for a shout-out, Mom.

Jonathan, Abraham, and Hannah: You are my life's grounding and grace.